MW01355380

LORRI—

WHAT AN AWESOME PERSON!

ENJOY

The Tale of Edgar Trunk

BOOK 1

The Grimy, Often Miserable Factory (That Was His Home)

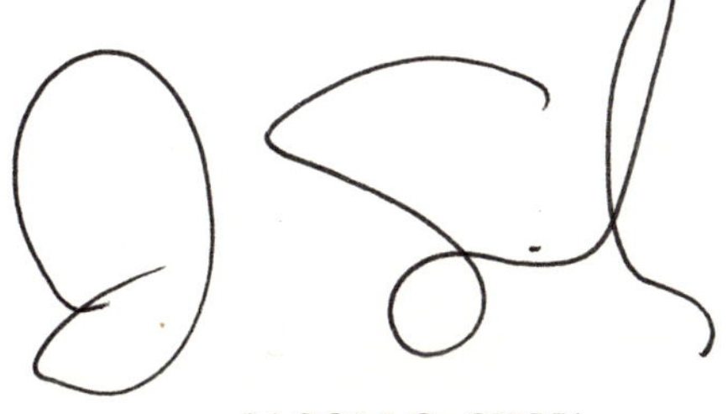

JASON O. SILVA

THIMBLE PUBLISHING
Los Angeles

9.29.12

This is a work of fiction. The events and characters described here are products of the author's imagination.

For information, address Thimble Publishing, 16733 Archwood Street, Los Angeles, CA 91406.

Email Queries: info@thimblepublishing.com

Thimble Publishing is a registered trademark.

Cover background water color artwork by James Teegarden.
Illustrations and Design by Mikie Pedersen.

ISBN 978-0-9831441-3-7

Library of Congress Control Number: 2010940684

10 9 8 7 6 5 4 3 2

For Heather

The Tale of Edgar Trunk

BOOK 1

The Grimy, Often Miserable Factory (That Was His Home)

1

THE MOST DISGUSTING PLACE ON EARTH

At the edge of the earth, a giant factory billowed soot and ash from its stacks, forever blotting out the sun. The island where the factory sat had not seen daylight in over a century. Instead of a bright blue ocean, a river of sludge oozed around it. Everything colorful had died in the toxic air, and outdoor walks had become fatal. Only the dreaded Crillows, a horrible crow-like creature, thrived among the trunks of dead trees, reason enough not to venture out.

The factory was just as gloomy on the inside. A maze of corridors filled the main floor. A dim yellow light illuminated green cobblestone walls and linoleum floors. Lining these halls were hundreds of imposing metal doors, all secured shut. Not even Leonidas Warnock could open them, despite repeated attempts. They opened and closed at will, if you asked him. It was like the place had a mind of its own.

Warnock was a large, brutish man who held the esteemed position of Official Operator of Sludge and Machine Parts, a job he took very seriously. He commanded a fleet of mechanical workers in the job of moving the toxic sludge around the factory and into rooms he had never seen.

In truth, he had seen few rooms. Whenever he got curious enough to investigate the place, mysterious gusts of air swooshed through the hallways slamming doors shut before he could glimpse inside. He could bend a steel bar into a pretzel, and he could beat any man to a pulp, but once the doors shut, even he was unable to budge them.

On this particular day, Warnock cared little about doors. He had awakened in the night to voices outside his workroom. Frightened, he roused the Assistant to the Official Operator of Sludge and Machine Parts and demanded that he check the halls for any "visitors." The Assistant was known as Stewpot due to his cylindrical head and a flat cap he never went without. Stewpot clambered out of bed in a daze. He bumped into the wall beside the door, and then into the door itself, before Warnock impatiently shoved him out. When Stewpot checked the hallway, he found nothing out of the ordinary and went back to bed, cap and all. Warnock on the other hand lay with one eye open the rest of the night. He had felt this way before. Exactly nine years ago, in fact. He shuddered thinking about the day *he* came to be under his charge.

Nine years ago, a package arrived at the factory door. It was sealed in protective wrapping to defend against the toxic air. Warnock had opened it in a craze, thrashing the outer layer to pieces and discarding the remains behind him. He hadn't expected the latest shipment of cream-filled pastries to arrive until the following week, and this was a pleasant surprise. When he got through the outer layer, his grin fell away. There were no pastries inside. Instead, he had unwrapped a perfect little man, a boy to be exact, Edgar Trunk.

Warnock despised many things. Most of all, he despised boys, all of whom he knew to be "unfit."

Edgar had just turned one year-old on the morning he arrived swaddled in protective clothing. Warnock would have tossed him out with the trash if the note in the boy's shirt hadn't warned against harming him. The front, written in black, read:

To: Uncle Warnock

Enclosed: Edgar Trunk

On the other side, the note said only:

Keep alive, at all costs, or you will be hunted down and killed by a creature worse than your most terrifying nightmares.

Horrible creatures plagued Warnock's dreams. He always slept with a night-light on because he had a strange feeling that the mysterious noises he heard in the halls, and the sudden gusts that kept him out of so many rooms, were no coincidence. He was stronger than any man, but creatures were a different story. Whatever he did, he had to keep the boy alive and the creatures at bay.

The task proved difficult because Warnock despised children. They were filthy vermin-carriers that managed to break everything valuable and make horrible siren sounds when beaten. But this child was different. The little boy toyed with his mind by keeping silent, even when Warnock hit him with a leather cargo strap, or forgot to feed him for a few days. No matter what Warnock did, the tiny little boy-man just stared at him with big brown eyes. They occasionally welled up with tears, but most of the time, they watched his every move. Warnock hated the sight of that gaze, of that boy. He put him to work in a miniscule room and avoided him.

And what was with the "Uncle" business in the note? Warnock didn't have any brothers or sisters. He did have an uncle of his own, an Uncle Virgil or something like that, a steelworker who disappeared into a mineshaft before Warnock was old enough to walk. But like his official position at work, "Uncle" was another title of respect, of which he fancied himself more than deserving. He decided he rather liked it, and if he were going to be addressed by a low-life brat, it would be as *Uncle* Warnock.

Nine years later, Edgar looked the same except he'd grown a little bigger. His straight brown hair came down to his eyebrows. His knobby knees and elbows were redder than the rest of him. His nose, a small point on his face, curved slightly to the left. In those nine years, Warnock's feelings toward him remained constant: Edgar Trunk was unfit for life, for work, and for breathing. His only job was to clean the numerous drain covers brought to him throughout the day, and although he never complained, he lacked enthusiasm, which Warnock understood to be a sign of ingratitude. If Warnock hadn't been so busy with his other duties, he would have given the job to one of his mechanical workers, but the boy had to do something. There is a saying about "idle hands" being the devil's plaything. Warnock certainly wasn't going to let a good-for-nothing little snot have a pair of those.

So, Edgar spent his days cleaning drain covers inside the 10 by 10 foot box he called his room. Although, a room has a bed full of pillows, colorful drapes over the windows, and a chest of drawers teeming with hand-me-downs from cousins that had outgrown them, not Edgar's. He slept on two crates pushed together. A pail of water sat in the corner for bathing. If he was lucky, his "Uncle" Warnock changed out the sponge. Most of the time he forgot, or deemed Edgar unfit for the day, holding back clean sponges for boys who were totally *un*-Edgar-like, even though there were no other boys in the factory.

There were also few people. Warnock, Stewpot, and Edgar were the only ones there, other than the mechanical workers, which Warnock alone saw, since he was the only certified operator of sludge and machine parts.

Warnock went to work each morning, going from his workroom, where he slept, to the sludge rooms, where he commanded the workers all day while eating cream pastries. He returned in time for dinner and a few hours of sleep before starting all over again the next day. Stewpot filled in the tasks of housekeeping, the occasional cooking—they mostly feasted on stale bread rolls saved by the millions in cabinets above the workroom—and other odds and ends. A quiet fellow, he took to entertaining Edgar whenever possible, and while he seldom said more than a few words at a time, the two became good friends.

Warnock didn't approve of friendships. In his mind, they were unprofessional and led to such troublesome things as anarchy and happiness. Ever since the boy had come to the factory, other matters occupied Warnock's thoughts. Strange voices echoed down the distant corridors. When he closed his eyes, he heard whispers outside his door. On Edgar's first night in the factory, Warnock stood with his workroom door cracked open. He peered through the slit and saw a cloaked figure heading toward the boy's room. When he opened the door and stepped out for a better look, the figure was gone. Warnock crept down the hallway to check Edgar's room. The boy was missing. Fearing the creature from the note, he retreated to his room and waited all night. He didn't sleep a wink, and on the way to the sludge rooms he stopped in again, and Edgar lay there dozing as if nothing had happened. He never saw the figure again.

Now, Edgar was ten years old. Nine years had passed since that frightful night, and the same uneasiness Warnock felt back then he felt now. In his dreams, strangers in cloaks surrounded him. Creatures tore him limb from limb. Crillows pecked out his eyes. Warnock slept with five locks on the door and two torch lights blazing. He sawed off the legs of his bed to make sure no creature could hide beneath it. Something odd was definitely in the air.

Edgar felt it, too. He never told his uncle, but the stranger in the cloak had haunted *his* dreams for years. Edgar tried to recall the entire scene, to conjure the image of the figure, but he couldn't get more than a flash, like a thought dashing out of view before he could catch it.

He sat before a stack of filthy drain covers in his room, behind on his work. The fragmented dreams consumed his attention, stalling him. In a corner, Stewpot played his favorite game, Balance the Broom. Stewpot stood the broom upright and balanced it on his palm. The broom started to tip over, and Stewpot lurched to the side to stay under it. The broom tipped back and Stewpot lurched back. He peered at Edgar, half-smiling, eager to catch a spark of amusement.

Edgar lifted the top cover and scraped at a wedge of gunk with his withered brush.

"Stewpot," he said. "I've had the dream again."

Stewpot's concentration was not to be broken. He gained confidence in his balancing and let the broom tip twice as far as before. The broom dropped, and Stewpot lurched farther than expected. Edgar reached forward, but too late—Stewpot's back foot slipped, tearing his legs into the splits.

"Stewpot!" he cried out.

Stewpot grimaced, his legs spread far apart.

"Are you okay?"

"Maybe," he whispered, unable to look Edgar in the eyes. He took the hem of his pants and began the process of righting his legs in front of his body, proof that he was fine. Edgar resumed his work. He held the back of his brush against the metal—the bristles had worn off ages ago—and planed a knot of gristle from the underside.

"I don't like those dreams. I feel empty after I've had them."

Stewpot chewed his lip, thinking, then said, "The cloak, Egger." He had trouble with the name, so Edgar was just "Egger."

"Yes, the stranger in the cloak. I haven't dreamt about him in a long time. But lately, every time I close my eyes, he's there."

Stewpot stood and stretched to his full lanky height. With a sigh, he dropped his shoulders to their usual slouched position, his body settling into a question mark.

"Something bad is going to happen—I can feel it."

"Like what?" Stewpot said.

"I'm not sure, but something funny is going on with the factory. Don't you ever wonder why we can only go to a few rooms? This place is humongous."

"Why would you want to?"

Edgar considered this. "I just think there has to be more than all these rooms and hallways."

"And Boss."

"Yes, and him," Edgar sighed.

Stewpot perked up. "Egger, I almost forgot." He reached under his jacket and took out a small package. Edgar immediately knew what it was.

"Another book! Where did you find it?"

"Dunno." Stewpot grinned so wide his crooked back teeth shown.

Edgar unwrapped the book, an ancient leather-bound tome titled: *How Big IS a Little Bigger?*

Suddenly, the door swung open and Uncle Warnock barged in. Edgar jammed the book under his shirt and pretended to be working.

"Why aren't these clean?" Warnock kicked the stack of drain covers across the room.

"Uncle, I've been working all morning," Edgar cried.

"Unfit! Unfit! Unfit!" he bellowed.

Edgar folded his arms over his shirt to keep the book from dropping into the open. "Sorry, Uncle! I'll work much faster."

Warnock wheezed through his narrow esophagus.

"To think," he said, drawing out a brand new brush full

of stiff, shiny bristles, "I was actually going to give you this."

"A new brush would be wonderful," Edgar beamed. "I could clean twice as many drains!"

"You don't deserve it. I'm not giving it to you. You are unfit for this brush."

Warnock stuffed the brush into his tunic and removed a pastry. He bit it in half, squirting yellow cream down his chin. He lashed it up with his fat whale tongue, ensnaring the goop, drawing it back into his mouth.

"Boy," he said through a mouthful of dough. "You are unfit . . . unfit for work, unfit for life, unfit for being."

A small glob remained in the corner of his mouth.

"I'm sorry, Uncle," Edgar said.

"What did you say, maggot?"

"I said…"

"You will stay in your cell!" he bellowed, then quickly corrected himself: "I mean, in your *room*. Even though you are unfit for your own room." He digressed, "I'll let you keep it—because I am not without mercy."

Warnock tossed a few morsels at Edgar's feet, which landed like rocks. "Take some bread—there'll be no stew for you this evening." He glared at the boy. "What's under your shirt?"

"Uncle, no."

"Stand UP!" he bellowed.

Edgar got to his feet, trembling, and the book fell onto the floor.

Warnock's eyes got as big as croquet balls. "WHAT is that? A BOOK!" He picked it up and held it above Edgar's head. "Books belong in the FIRE! You know what else I ought to put in the fire?" Warnock backed Edgar against the wall.

There was a clatter behind Warnock—Stewpot had smacked his broom against the floor.

Warnock turned to him. "You stupid oaf! Get out of here."

He got right in his face, breathing heavily, but Stewpot didn't budge.

"Are you deaf? Eh? Are you dumb?"

Warnock shoved the last of his pastry into his tunic and pushed the sleeves up his burly arms. Stewpot's knees knocked together, his eyes welled up, but he stood his ground. Warnock grinned, a look proclaiming he knew just how to handle this situation.

"You're sleeping in the corridor tonight," he said. "And you know what else you're gonna get?" He raised his fist into the air.

"Uncle," Edgar shouted. "CRILLOWS!"

Warnock's shoulders collapsed. His fist fell away.

"What?"

Edgar's lips quivered.

"Crillows, Uncle—I saw one go by—its feet were awful."

Warnock stared at Edgar.

"You…saw them? You're sure?"

"They had wretched feet, with scary old toenails hanging off."

"No…"

"Yes. I can hear them right now. Those feet slapping down the hallway."

"Can't be. Not inside the factory."

"Yes…" Edgar croaked.

Warnock stood with his ear facing the door. Stewpot looked as if he were about to faint.

Warnock stopped listening for Crillow feet. His hands balled up into fists. He leaned toward Edgar, his face full of suspicion. Edgar felt helpless in the blast of his uncle's breath—it reeked of spoiled eggs and lemon cream. *This is it*, he thought. *I am done for.*

Suddenly, a frenzied slapping sound filled the room.

Warnock straightened up. His bottom lip trembled. A ripple of panic spread through his body, and he fled the room, squealing in a pitch very unbecoming for a man.

When he was gone, Edgar turned to Stewpot and said, "Crillows, huh?"

Stewpot shrugged. Holding the broom, he slapped it against the palm of his hand, creating the same sound that had sent Warnock into a tizzy.

The two of them smiled from ear to ear recalling Warnock's girlish wail as he'd fled—and all because of Stewpot slapping a broom with his hand.

"Well, thank goodness you didn't go for that awful death wail—only a real Crillow can make that noise."

Stewpot grew solemn.

"Can it really do that?" Edgar inquired. "Can it really drive a person to madness?"

Stewpot raised his hands into the air, miming a scary creature of some sort.

"Like a wraith? How do you know?"

He shrugged again—he just *knew*. He turned and left the room, closing the door on the way out. Stewpot always came and went without warning. It was just his way. Edgar, left alone, sat down on the floor and picked up another drain cover.

There was nothing else for him to do. He had no special magic he could call upon to save him. There were no mysterious or even imagined friends to steal him away to some paradise. There were no toys and no televisions; no jungle gyms or swings; no candies or cakes (these were for Uncle Warnock only); no mothers or fathers; no stars and no sun. There was the factory and his life inside it. On the morning of Edgar's tenth birthday he was unaware that he had lived for an entire decade. He had no concept of time, days, weeks, months, certainly not years, while inside the fortress of a factory. Since there were no clocks and no calendars, since neither sun nor star shown through the blanketed smog, and since there was no daylight or moonlight, Edgar could not have known that another year had passed.

But all that was about to change, because something funny *was* going on in the factory, not the least of which was a sudden and alarming knock. Not just any knock.

A very, very loud knock.

Warnock didn't hear it. After leaving Edgar's room, he had hurried to bed, fastened all five locks on his door, and stuffed cloth into his ears. Two blazing torches filled his room with blinding light. Quick to bed, he tucked a stuffed giraffe under his arm, one he'd stolen from Stewpot, and climbed under the covers. He needed one good night's rest without strange voices outside his door, or nightmares of cloaked strangers and Crillows. For once, he would get it. Warnock plummeted into deep sleep. His hulking body slowly rolled to the side, squeezing the giraffe's button eye-ball off with a pop.

2

THE DOOR IN THE CORRIDOR

KNOCK!

KNOCK!

KNOCK!

A bomb had gone off—that's what it sounded like—three bombs in a row. Edgar stood, toppling over his stack of drain covers.

KNOCK!

KNOCK!

KNOCK!

He flinched with each beat.

The room fell quiet again, save the ringing in Edgar's ears. Where was Uncle Warnock in all this commotion? He figured whatever was out there was probably much bigger than he was. He braced for the sound again.

He waited. Bits of stone lay on the floor, shaken from the crevices. Suddenly, another knock—this one more … distant. Edgar was perplexed. He had no idea what was making the noise. He listened for it, but there was only silence for a long time.

Slowly, he stepped toward the door. Maybe he had guessed wrong—maybe the knocking had come from farther away than his room. Over the years, he had glimpsed rooms filled with enormous machine parts—gears, cogs, and sprockets. Even though he'd never heard anything like it before, Edgar believed a machine like that could have made the noise. He really did not know what secrets the factory contained—anything was possible.

Each day, Warnock disappeared through a particular set of doors not too far away from his workroom. Edgar had tried to sneak in behind him but they always shut before he could slip in, and all he ever saw was another dark hallway.

Gusts of wind often filled the corridors, slamming doors, whistling against the lights on the ceiling. Edgar hated them—they were like ghosts. He had read a book called *Marge McGinty Crosses Over*. It began:

She up and died while eating fruit pie,
And quite large was Marge that
The Heavenly light gave a good fight,
But in the end, she just was too fat.

The book went on to tell the story of large Marge McGinty, who was so big she couldn't get to heaven when she died, and so remained in her home for eternity, left to haunt the empty rooms. Edgar imagined the factory chock full of Marge McGintys muttering between the walls, chatting each other up outside his room while he slept, and most of all, zipping through the corridors sealing off rooms before he could fully inspect them.

The factory could be a lonely place with its endless hallways and doors. Discovering ghosts in the factory would not surprise Edgar one bit. Like the voices he often heard—creepy, nonsensical whispers—strange sounds were nothing new to him. In all his years, Edgar had heard everything. But he'd never heard the knocking sound. He opened his door and peered into the corridor. It was empty.

One thing never changed: the persistent feeling that he was being watched. Conscious of the walls, or ghosts, or whatever might be hiding from him, Edgar stepped into the hallway to investigate the mysterious knocking.

He looked down the hallway. The door to Warnock's workroom was wide open. "That's strange," he thought. "Warnock never leaves his door open."

Had he or Stewpot been hurt? He rushed toward the room. "Uncle? Mr. Stewpot?" He jumped over the heap of blankets in the corridor where Stewpot had slept the night before, wheeled around the doorway, and stopped. No one was there. Aside from the occasional glimpse, it was the first time he'd been able to observe his uncle's chamber.

Like everything else in the factory, Warnock's workroom was quite plain. His legless bed frame occupied the majority of the space, its middle permanently sunken. Two torches blazed bright. Stewpot's much smaller bed, stripped to the mattress, was off to the side. A few rickety dressers lined the far wall, and a row of tall cabinets that stored the bread rolls hung above them. Edgar recalled his night without stew and thought of delighting in just a few more to satisfy his hunger. Better not, he thought. If Warnock caught him, he'd be made into mincemeat. On the other hand...

Edgar's gaze fell upon a small potbelly stove in the corner. The remains of the book Stewpot had given him lay smoldering. Countless other books had burned there over the years. Warnock loathed books and reading, with the exception of books that had pictures of machines and pretty women posing with machines. Edgar never had a picture book—he had to rely on his imagination, another thing Warnock despised.

He didn't think it was wise to linger in front of Warnock's room. Edgar looked down the corridor in the direction of his own room. He looked the other way where he presumed the mysterious knocking sound had come from. Against his better judgment, he decided to investigate the corridors before returning to the stack of drain covers waiting to be cleaned.

Edgar tiptoed down the hallway staying close to the wall, even though there was no place to hide should he run into his uncle. He kept an ear out for the knocking.

Because there were no distinguishing marks in the corridors or on any of the doors, no one could go far without feeling utterly lost. No one except Edgar. He may not have seen inside the many rooms, he may not have had a great deal of free time to do as he pleased, but over the years he had mentally logged miles of corridors. It was his only freedom. Since Warnock despised Edgar, since he would rather see a cockroach do a jig on the tip of his nose than look at an unfit good-for-nothing wretch, Edgar spent hours alone. Except for the usual visits, when he received additional drain covers and a few bread rolls, he hardly saw his uncle. The work was demanding, and he didn't have the luxury of falling short of Warnock's exorbitant daily quota of clean covers, but there were plenty of hiccups. Five minutes here. Fifteen minutes there. A sleepless night. Edgar had put these moments to use exploring.

He moved quickly, quietly along. The maze of corridors consumed him. Some straight as an arrow, some curved, some leading to dead ends. He navigated his way to the place farthest from his room before the corridors circled back on each other, leading him toward the start again.

He covered as much ground as he could without going through a door, and still no trace of the sound. Edgar sulked.

"Probably imagined it," he said.

But then a curious thing happened: the knocking returned.

It came from a corridor to his left. Edgar stepped toward that direction—KNOCK! He took another step—KNOCK!

He paused as an unsettling quiet lingered in the corridors. No knock.

He moved again, and the sound returned, clearer and closer. It called to him. Edgar's heart beat with excitement. When he moved down the hall, the knocking continued. If he stopped, it stopped. The sound was guiding him.

Edgar followed the knocking for miles, exhilarated. He was so entranced with the mystery of the sound that he lost his bearings. He wound around bends and passed through countless intersecting corridors until he realized he was totally lost. He paused. His stomach suddenly twisted into knots as he pictured Warnock stopping by his room and finding him missing. Two knocks rang out impatiently. "Sorry," Edgar replied. He shook off the worry and followed.

The knocking sound, at first louder than a jackhammer, was now soft and unassuming, like a whisper. The noise had all but disappeared, and Edgar slowed his search, becoming cautious. Had he finally reached his destination?

The hall where he ended up appeared no different from the rest. Then Edgar spotted something.

He moved toward the wall and knelt down. Hidden in the shadows, no higher than Edgar's chest, was a squat wooden door. A sign hung above it, proclaiming: NO ONE SHALL ENTER.

In all his exploring, miles and miles of corridors tracked and memorized, he'd only seen large heavy metal doors. How had he missed one like this?

Edgar backed away, glanced in either direction down the corridor to see if he'd been followed. Satisfied he was alone, he returned to the door that promised, "No one shall enter."

He squinted in the dim light, reading more closely. "That's strange," he blurted in surprise. Had he misread? There was no space between the first two words. It really said: NOONE SHALL ENTER.

Edgar was sure it had said "No One" just a moment ago. He checked the corridor again. Was someone playing a trick on him?

After a long while, he reached for the knob.

"Oh!" He drew back. "It's ice cold."

Edgar peered down at four frosty fingerprints.

Baffled by his discovery, Edgar did not hear the foot-steps clacking down the hallway. Then a voice rang out, breaking his concentration, "Wretched, unfit little thing."

Edgar freaked—his uncle! He was so turned around he couldn't tell which direction the voice came from.

"Unfit, unfit, unfit," it sang. The only thing Edgar was sure of was that his uncle was getting closer. Soon enough, he'd come wheeling round the bend, find him outside his room, and crucify him.

Like a sneeze, "Un-, un-, un-, UN-FIT!"

Edgar went with his instincts. He bent down to the small wooden door, gripped the icy knob, and opened it. A chilling blast of air escaped from a dark, shadowy passageway inside.

"Little-wittle wretchigans," Uncle Warnock coughed, right on his heels. Edgar crawled into the passage and pushed the door shut behind him. Still as a ghost, he held his breath.

A tremor of panic moved through him as the heavy footsteps clacked nearby and paused right outside the door.

This is surely it, he thought. I've been found out.

But the footsteps started up again, this time fading into the distance.

Edgar collapsed with a sigh of relief. He leaned against the back of the door. It was ice!

Despite the warmth of the passage, the slab of ice covering the door showed no signs of melting. Edgar ran his hands along it, intrigued. He'd read all about ice in a book called *Cold Hard Things*, learned about glaciers, avalanches, and a large machine named The Titanic. He never thought he'd actually get to touch ice. He turned toward the long passage before him, excited, wondering what other mysteries lie beyond.

He stood up—the tunnel was just his size—and stooped slightly just to ensure he didn't bump his head. He laughed, imagining Warnock trying to follow him. The image of his uncle attempting to squeeze his fat hulking figure past the wooden door was hilarious.

He ventured farther down the passage, his curiosity burning. After all the years of wanting to go beyond the metal doors of the factory, he'd never imagined this. The wooden door baffled him. And he didn't have a clue as to what to make of the sign. Or the ice!

Edgar traveled a long way down the tunnel, stopping only once, when he thought he heard a voice. He was accustomed to hearing voices, but this was different. It had called his name with a sort of hiss:

"*Ed-ghhurr..!*"

He listened. It was so quiet even his breathing sounded amplified. Edgar dismissed the notion, thinking he'd only imagined the sound. Farther on, he did hear the murmur of a human voice. It was far off in the distance and was accompanied by another sound, the soft whoosh of air.

No, it can't be, he thought. But sure enough, although very faint, he detected Uncle Warnock's barking. Edgar pushed ahead, thinking he was finally going to get the chance to see his uncle at work.

Behind him, a shadow slipped down from the ceiling and filled the passageway. Two dark yellow eyes shimmered, and a slithery voice hissed with the trace of a smile:

"*That'ssss ... a* good *boy*!"

And while Edgar was far ahead of the shadow by then, he did have the strange sensation that someone, or some *thing*, was following him.

3

THE WIND IN THE BILLOWS

Edgar followed the dark passageway to its end, exiting through a squat door that went to his waist, and entered into a large hollow.

A steady current of warm air tousled his hair. A luminous glow, its source difficult to pinpoint, revealed the eliptical shape of the room. It was fifty feet to the opposite wall, but the ceiling stretched twice as high above, where several dozen openings breathed air into the hollow.

Warnock's voice rang out above the whoosh of air, "You're no better than unfit toilet vermin … less fit than rodent droppings!" His voice came from the vents, the air brandishing his words with an echo. The distance did not appear to have an effect on his volume. Edgar couldn't tell how far or near his uncle was.

"The hose, the hose, you unfit cretin!" he bellowed. "The sludge has to flow free. Have you forgotten the sludge, you sack of donkey dung? Eh, have you?" He was very particular, "The *sludge* must *flow*! It's why we're here!"

Uncle Warnock maintained his rigorous berating like an Olympian. It was "vermin" this or "unfit" that. His barking penetrated the whooshing air inside the hollow with ease, as Edgar tried to make sense of the strange commands. It was no secret that Warnock was the Official Operator of Sludge and Machine Parts, and that he worked in the sludge rooms, but the details ended there. He kept his work private. The only time he mentioned sludge was in a threatening way, like the time he insisted Edgar would have to eat sludge for supper if he kept looking at him in that condescending way. Or like the time he told him that all he wanted for his birthday was to toss Edgar into the river outside the factory. It was full of sludge.

For as long as Edgar could remember, Warnock had only shown concern for his well being once. Several years ago, he made them practice an evacuation. He, Edgar, and Stewpot had to pull masks over their heads, strap oxygen tanks to their backs, and go running down the corridor screaming, "Sky's fallin'! Sky's fallin'!" The drill ended abruptly when Stewpot passed out from the excitement.

Edgar had been the opposite of excited. The funny-tasting mask was awful, and the oxygen tanks were heavy. He had hardly been able to run beneath the weight of one. Afterward, he told Stewpot, if he never had to wear another funny tasting mask and bear the burden of those heavy tanks, it would be quite all right by him.

"Careful with that hose! Watch the sludge!" Uncle Warnock's tremendous voice echoed in the chamber. "Line up the hoses with the troughs, and not my stinkin' shoes, maggots! Easy with that! The bilge hose—watch the bilge hose!"

Edgar listened curiously to the way his uncle spoke commanding the fleet of workers—workers Warnock often alluded to as "the ones far superior to an unfit brat whose name rhymes with 'Fedgar.'" Edgar realized, quite simply, when one trimmed off all the details and all the unknowns about him, sludge was Warnock's job.

He chuckled. Didn't sound so great to him. Edgar stepped toward the center of the room and heard an audible *click!*

Suddenly the room was plunged into darkness. A quick, shrill alarm sounded.

It was the most awful noise he'd ever heard, a sound like metal churning against metal. It continued to fill his head with intense pain. One eye rolled back, while the other felt like it was going to pop.

The alarm stopped.

Edgar lay frozen, his heart pounding like a jackhammer, his ears ringing. He had somehow ended up on the floor, curled into a ball. His uncle's voice returned, sounding even angrier than normal.

"I said, *off* with that wretched alarm! Idiot! Check the air vents—somethin's triggered it." He paused before saying with a hint of fear, "Might be Crillows sneaking through the ventilation. Eh … you better look into it."

At once, tinny drumming roared into the hollow. The acoustics sounded louder than before, and the hollow felt stuffy. The air current! It must have shut off when the lights went out and the alarm sounded. Without it, the noise of a thousand tiny claws scraping and tapping at the ducts was amplified. He imagined Warnock's fleet of mechanized workers—whatever *they* looked like—scouring the ventilation paths. Then it hit him—

The ventilation. His uncle had demanded his fleet to look into the ventilation, and he was right at the heart of it all.

Warnock exploded, "The billows! The billows! Turn on the billows—do you want us to all die?"

A loud *clat-a-tat-vroooom!* rushed into the hollow—an engine firing up nearby. After a moment's delay, the draft returned, stronger than before, whipping Edgar's hair. The light, however, remained off. He was left in the dark.

The tinny thrum of mechanical feet sounded more distant. Edgar breathed easier. Maybe they weren't headed for him.

He stood back up. He wasn't sure that what he had heard were mechanical feet, but the thought sent a shiver down his spine. Whatever they were, there were hundreds of them. And the hollow itself, with its vortex of warm air and echoing sound, reminded him of a book he read recently called *The Fire Inside* by Rosalie Cummins. It was all about fire and furnaces used to melt glass. The people who used them were known as glass blowers, and they were very particular about controlling the fire and heat, and had to introduce ventilation to direct the heat into cooling chambers so they didn't burn themselves into cinders. The air, the heat, Warnock's mention of billows—it all made sense to Edgar. The hollow must have been some sort of cooling chamber, which explained the warm and forceful air. And all those vents up high—

From somewhere in the darkness above, he heard the faint but unmistakable scratching of a lone set of feet.

Not a moment later, there was another set.

And another, and another … an entire army of mechanical feet approaching, resonating in the hollow in a cacophony of tinny drumbeats.

Edgar hurriedly backed away feeling for the wall in the dark, while images of his pursuers filled his head. He imagined tiny, coppery little machines with large chomping fangs and beady eyes.

The drumming beat of claws was *deafening*. He found the wall, but not the exit. Edgar groped maddeningly along a grimy plate of metal in search of the passage he had come from. The sound was disorienting, like having your head stuck inside the largest bee hive on Earth—with the queen bee before you, angered and threatened and pointing her bee scepter right at your nose, shouting for her drones to, "*Atttaaaaaackk*!"

Suddenly it was quiet except for the whoosh of air. Edgar didn't like this. He slowly turned and put his back against the wall. He thought he saw a set of beady red eyes glowing in the distance, and panicked.

The eyes paused, two tarnished evil rubies suspended in the blackness; they narrowed in on him. He was not imagining this. The glowing red dots grew bigger then smaller, honing in on their prey—him.

Edgar choked back a scream. The swirling air felt suffocating. *Please*, he thought, *oh, please just leave me alone. I promise I'll never come here again.*

The thing began to move toward him. Its feet tapped lightly on the floor, each footfall sending a jolt of fear down his spine. Where were the others? He stared at the approaching eyes. They were still far away—he guessed the creature had come down along the far wall. He still had time to find the exit. Edgar inched along the wall, keeping his eye on the creature

The creature stopped. Edgar thought maybe it had

changed its mind, but the eyes quivered and continued to advance on him.

Tip ... tap ... tip ... tap... It got close enough for Edgar to make out a slight mechanical whirring of machine parts.

High up in a corner across the chamber, a second pair of tarnished ruby eyes appeared, glanced in his direction, and dropped to the ground with a heavy metallic *cur-lunk!*

In horror he squinted through the dark to observe as another set followed—*cur-lunk!*—and another. *Cur-lunk!* Whatever chance of escape Edgar had had against a lone creature no longer mattered. The whole pack had found him.

Cur-lunk! Cur-lunk!

Edgar wanted to scream. He might have, too, if the whole nightmare had felt real. No, this was all too *un*real. *Cur-lunk! Cur-lunk!* They were dropping down in pairs, forming a mob across the blackness. Their eyes were like evil stars in a moonless sky, studying him. Eerily, a hundred eyes produced enough light in the dark for him to make out the creatures' true shapes.

Edgar gasped in terror. They were praying mantises.

If ever there was an appropriate time to scream, now

was it. But he didn't scream. He could hardly breathe. If he *had* screamed, he might not have heard a soft voice call out from beside him, "Psssst … you there…"

Edgar didn't even turn around. His gaze was fixed upon the mass of mechanical praying mantises before him, their hungry beady eyes, their long notched arms dancing maniacally in the air, anticipating their next move.

"You … over here now unless you want to be ripped apart."

This got his attention. Edgar sidled toward the voice on his left. Something pinched his ankle.

"Down here. You're going to have to crawl."

Edgar squatted down and felt the jagged opening of a crawlspace. He dove inside as fast as he could.

The mechanical mantises didn't like this one bit. With a forceful beat of legs against the floor and an annoyed sawing of their notched limbs—*ricket-ricket-ricket*—the mob rushed toward him.

"Hold on," the voice assured. Edgar heard the turning of rusty metal wheels, while the glowing eyes lit up a steel grate as it slid down to block them out. The first tried to stop, but was pushed from behind—*whack!*—slamming head first into the grate, falling. A dozen more rammed into it, falling on and crushing each other. One long notched arm poked through the bars, scratching Edgar on the leg.

"Oh!" he exclaimed.

"Come on, come on," the stranger urged.

"Who are you? Why are you helping me?"

"Shhhh," the voice said. "Not yet." A soft tap on the walls. "They're listening." The mantises were in a frenzy—*ricket-ricket-ricket*—their mechanical heads flailing about, their notched limbs sawing.

Ahead of Edgar, the stranger's feet slapped against the grime on the tunnel floor. Edgar tried to stand but banged his head. This passage was even smaller than the one he'd taken through the mysterious wooden door.

"Almost there," the voice said.

Almost where? Edgar wondered.

The faster he pushed on, the farther behind he seemed to be. *Slap, slap, slap*—the feet or hands or whatever belonged to the mysterious voice moved steadily and quickly.

Edgar smacked face-first into a wall, crying out, more from surprise than pain.

"Oh, do be careful." The voice was apologetic. "That's

the only turn. Not much farther now." Getting ahead again, "Not much farther at all."

Without knowing why, Edgar trusted his guide. He found that following in the dark wasn't so difficult as long as he listened for the slapping. Occasionally, the stranger paused long enough to say:

"Really, not *too* much farther."

Edgar wanted to bring up the fact that he'd said "not much farther" a very long time ago. The more ground they covered, the safer he felt. The mechanical mantises must have been a mile behind them now.

"Where are we going?" he got up the courage to ask. But the stranger did not answer him. Soon, a light entered the tunnel from up ahead. Edgar squealed with joy, pressing on quicker, before he realized the stranger was nowhere to be seen. He stopped in alarm.

"Keep on moving, big guy," the voice was behind him now.

"How did you get..?"

"No time, no time," the stranger urged. "Onward."

Edgar caught a whiff of something foul. "That smell," he hissed in disgust. "What is it?"

After he said it, Edgar felt a pinch in the rump.

"Don't," the stranger warned. His voice conveyed total fear.

"What is it?"

"Just don't ever do that. Don't—" a hesitation. "Don't hiss like that. Only true evil hisses. Please move along—almost there."

"But, wait. I didn't hiss."

"You did. You said, 'That ssssssmell.'"

"I'm sorry," Edgar said. "I didn't mean it. Only, the smell *is* awful."

"Oh, the smell is quite awful," he replied matter-of fact. "We're near some sludge reserves." Then, with a darker tone, "What's that got to do with hissing, though?"

"I'm very sorry," he said. "I shouldn't have done that."

"It's quite alright, Young Sir. You just have to be careful in this place."

"What … what did you call me?"

"Young Sir?"

Without warning, Edgar began to cry.

"Oh, dear. Have I offended you in some way, because I didn't mean to. It's just we need to get out of here. And if you really want to be safe—I certainly want to get us as far from those things as possible."

"No," Edgar said. "I'm sorry. I don't know what that was all about. I'm all right."

They pressed on in silence, the stranger following.

"So sorry," the stranger said after a while. "I didn't mean at all what you think I meant. You see, I am usually quite careful about this sort of thing, and I can be quite charming, I should add—at least I've been told that more than a few times."

"I'm okay, really."

The stranger continued to mutter to himself. Up ahead, Edgar saw a grate similar to the one that had saved them from the mantises. His heart jumped. He made out the outline of a metal door. After mechanical predators and slime and grime and alarms, those boring old halls were a welcoming sight. He'd stay in them forever if it meant never having to return to this awful secret stuff, and hissing strangers—*that* was a thing Edgar hoped most of all to forget.

The tunnel broadened. Edgar thought this a perfect opportunity to glimpse his new friend, who still jabbered away in a voice too soft to be understood. Carefully, so as not to frighten him, Edgar peered over his shoulder. He couldn't see his rescuer, but the light from the grate spread down the passageway, shining on the murky goo on the walls. He cringed to think what his hands and knees looked like.

Edgar dropped his shoulder and craned his neck farther to check closer to the floor; perhaps his new friend had resorted to crawling on hands and knees. He turned a little more, ignoring the mounting pain in his shoulder.

Still, no glimpse.

There was no more finessing the point. Edgar rolled onto his rump and sat facing down the passageway. As he plopped down in the grime, the stranger swallowed his sentence and darted back into the shadows.

"Wha-what are you doing? I don't like it. Please just move along."

The stranger was so artfully hidden now that not even a creature of the night could make him out. But his quickness in the tunnel and his awareness of the dark were no even match against the element of surprise. He had reacted a fraction of a second too late. That's when Edgar saw it—

not much, but enough to feed his imagination—one tiny, narrow beak.

"What are you?"

"Excuse me," the creature said. "But are you laughing at me?"

"I guess I am," Edgar chuckled.

"That isn't nice, you know."

"I am sorry. I know it isn't nice. It's just…" Edgar broke off in silence.

"No, go ahead. I don't mean to discourage you."

Edgar mulled over the creature's words. "You're very nice, is all. And I haven't laughed in a very long time."

Now each of them sat still—Edgar in the soft light from the corridors, the creature under cover of shadow.

Two hearts thrummed inside two small chests, and each beat with excitement, fear, and something else unknown to them both. Finally, the creature spoke, his words ushered forth with the utmost gravity.

"Young Sir," he said, "we haven't much time. The big round fella will not be happy when he finds you gone. He *will* find you gone, by the way. You must do exactly as he says. Do not give him any other reason to be cruel to you.

He will not harm you, I promise. The penalty against him will be too grave. He has strict instructions never to lay a hand on you. I can't explain—you just have to trust me. But do not provoke him. A fella like that is too delicately attached in the brain.

"Now, there is so little that you know and so much that you cannot fathom. I am not the one to explain this to you, or to tell you the things you do not know. I'm just a friend. If I've done my job, we'll never meet again. Know this: I cannot save you if you decide to venture through the wooden door again. It's far too dangerous. What I will say is this: there's a whole world of power in your name. The meaning of this will come to you in time.

"Instructions. You must do exactly as I say for your own good, and for the good of many others. Ahead is a grate; I will open it for you so you can exit into the corridor. When you get out, go directly to your right. In the floor, you will notice the number 3. It's very small, and time has caused its bright blue face to fade. If you look closely, though, you will see it. Follow the threes until you reach the main corridor. Go straight to your room. Wait there.

Do not venture out. Do not argue when the big fella comes for you. Only nod your head. I promise, he will not strike you. He values his life far too much.

"I'm not saying you needn't worry, though. Take aim, and always beware the hiss. There are things in this place that want you dead. I wish it weren't so, but this is a warning you need take to heart. There's IT … and there's HIM. I pray you never meet either—especially HIM. IT is horrible and wicked … but HIM … HIM's the devil himself.

"One last thing. You likely have a thousand questions right now. That's okay. Questions make the universe go."

There was a sound like thread breaking, and a small velvet pouch emerged from the shadow and plopped down between Edgar's legs.

"Now, take this. Open it only when you are alone. Its contents are for your eyes only. I'm not exactly saying there's magic in there—certainly it doesn't seem that way. Anyhow, you will know what to do. And please, Edgar…"

"What is it?"

There was no answer.

The creature had gone. A moment later, Edgar heard

the turning of rusty metal wheels, and the grate rose up. He took a deep breath, grabbed the pouch, and headed out of the tunnel.

4

THE CREATION STONES

Edgar was so excited to be out of the horrid tunnels that he walked a hundred feet before remembering to look for threes in the floor.

He had never paid any attention to the floor, but when he knelt down he discovered an intricate marbling of hues: deep purple, chocolate brown, slate gray, and maroon. It was smooth and cool to the touch, worn dull over the ages.

He scoured every inch of linoleum within sight, but no blue threes.

Edgar removed the little pouch from his pocket. It was soft and velvety, cinched shut, and secured with a knot. Edgar knew a thing or two about knots thanks to his uncle. One of Warnock's biggest annoyances was Edgar's shoes.

From time to time, Warnock was forced to find new

shoes for Edgar whenever his feet outgrew the ones he had. The first few times this happened, he simply cut the tips of them right off, so Edgar's toes poked out. He didn't care about the floppy soles, which had worn away to nothing, or the heel without padding, which caused painful blisters. Edgar could run around without shoes for all Warnock cared. But if he expected the brat to do any work, he figured he had to have something on his feet. Problem was, Edgar's feet seemed to grow much quicker these days. Warnock found himself replacing the shoes every few months. He was starting to think Edgar purposely did something to make his feet bigger, something spiteful to anger and annoy him.

Eventually, he gave in. He found an old pair of work boots, which were stiff as metal, and let the conniving, unfit rodent figure out the rest. Edgar took the boots thankfully. His old ones were in such disrepair that he could only get them to stay on by wrapping up the pieces in a strip of cloth and binding them to his feet with rope. However, the new shoes presented a different dilemma. He could only secure the firm material to his ankle by pulling the laces tight and knotting them two and three times over.

At the end of the day, Edgar had the task of untying the knots, which at first was grueling and caused his fingertips to burn, but now was thoughtless and second nature. So, Edgar was assured that he could open the velvety bag with ease, even though the stranger had been very specific about doing that only in the safety of his room.

A little peek wouldn't hurt, Edgar thought to himself. Who would know?

But he caught the glimmer of an eye studying him, or what seemed like an eye, and felt a pang of guilt. The creature had saved his life. The least he could do was follow his advice.

He shuddered as he recalled the evil of which the stranger spoke. Could there possibly be others in the factory who wanted him dead? And what had he meant about finding great power in his name?

"Edgar Trunk," he whispered. "Doesn't sound so powerful."

He glimpsed that staring eye again—a small sparkle. His heart beat like crazy as he moved toward it and knelt down for a closer look.

Amid all the swirling reds and browns, there was one

deep blue smudge. When he looked closer, he saw it was more than a smudge. Embedded in the worn marbled floor was the number three.

Now that he was aware of it, Edgar saw the three clear as day, as if it gave off its own light. He looked up, and a prominent trail of blue appeared, stretching down the hallway, sparkling like jewels.

Edgar thought gleefully, so *this* is what the stranger meant.

He slipped the velvet pouch into his pocket and, feeling exuberant, Edgar floated down the hallway. He followed the trail back to his room, swung the door wide open, but came to a sudden halt. His glee ended there. Uncle Warnock leaned against his wall, arms crossed angrily, waiting for him.

"Look at you—just filthy. Get in here. Quickly."

Edgar obeyed. His legs shook so badly he was lucky to still be standing. *He will not harm you, I promise*, the stranger had said. *He will not strike you*. But where was the stranger now? Edgar's uncle looked more terrifying than ever, towering over him.

The stench of his sweaty armpits was awful—sugar

and sour milk. His breath reeked of the foulest dumpster ever recorded—as envisioned in the story *Dirk's Dump*, not one of Edgar's favorites—and with each grunt and bellow, the big ogre blasted Edgar's face with hot putrid air.

"I told you never to leave this room. Never to go out into the corridors. They are off-limits. *OFF*-LIMITS. You, you wretched little thing, are unfit to walk them. Unfit to breathe the air and eat our food."

Edgar kept his back straight and his head down. He wanted to cry, but fought it off. *Just nod your head and be silent*, the stranger had advised. Edgar tried to nod, even though his head felt like it weighed a thousand pounds right now.

Trying not to let his thoughts go wild, Edgar focused on the gruesome details of his uncle's body. Warnock's folded arms were beastly. They seemed as thick around as Edgar's entire body. His hairy flesh was ruddy and permanently stained brown. His large callused hands contained ten beefy fingers and eight yellow fingernails—two were missing, a soft spongy type of skin in their place. Edgar moved on from the hands before he got too sick, coming to his uncle's belly. It was so rotund the gigantic cloth of his tunic contained only half of it. His deep bellybutton stuck out for all to see, cloaked in a swath of curls.

Edgar caught sight of his own body, which was covered in tar black gunk, and was so surprised that he gasped.

Warnock mistook the noise. "Are you talking back!" he barked.

Don't look him in the face, Edgar thought. *Nod. Nod away.*

"I'm talking to you, boy. Tell me what you said, or I'll crush your pathetic little fingers."

Warnock raised his hand to strike him. "ANSWER ME!"

Nodding was not going to make this go away. Edgar collapsed to the floor in tears. "Please, don't, Sir, please don't hit me."

Warnock held his gigantic hairy arm poised, bearing a look Edgar knew well. The look said he was ready to crush this pathetic excuse of a boy in a single blow.

Edgar shielded his face, awaiting it.

Warnock only chuckled. "You have drain covers to clean before you can eat." He left Edgar cowering on the floor and slammed the door on his way out, locking it.

Edgar felt some relief. That was a close one. The only reason he'd reacted during Warnock's rampage was that he hadn't recognized himself. His hands, caked in grime, were two giant gloves of muck. His clothes looked like clumps of worm guts. He had no idea it would be this disgusting.

Edgar rolled onto his side. The encounter with Uncle Warnock, the mechanical mantises, the miles of filthy tunnel he had crawled—all had drained him. For once, the cold touch of the cement felt soothing. He need only close his eyes to pass into oblivion and dream, dream, dream.

Edgar was sure of one thing: his dreams would not be happy ones. He spread out flat on the floor, and something shifted in his pocket. The pouch! He was too weak to move a single muscle, but he nearly smiled. Perhaps there was a little hope in his miserable world. And with that thought, he slipped into the deepest kind of rest.

Edgar awoke the next day rejuvenated. Someone had been in his room. He saw a large pail full of water and a coarse sponge. The dried grime on his hands crumbled away in large hunks as he gripped the pail and moved it against the wall. He noticed a small crate sitting in a corner of the room. The lid had shifted sideways. He slid it open—two dried bread rolls and a pot of cold soup. He was famished.

He plunged his filthy hands into the refreshing ice-cold water. He scrubbed his arms and neck and face. Without the tunnel grime he began to feel more like himself. Now, food.

He took the soup in one hand, held the roll in his mouth, and flipped the crate onto its side so he could use it as a bench. A single yellow light bulb flickered above him. Edgar felt good. It was the morning after his run-in with Uncle Warnock. And he had survived! Things were looking up for poor old Edgar Trunk. There's *power* in that name. He felt quite big for such small britches, and with a full belly, he sauntered across the room for a bit of exercise. When he stood, he felt the pouch in his pocket.

He took it out and ran his fingers over the knot. Now was the time. He nimbly undid the knot and opened it.

A burst of colorful light nearly blinded him.

When his eyes adjusted, he saw that his dimly lit room was awash with a rainbow of light spilling out of the pouch. It tossed hundreds of swirling stars onto the ceiling.

"What *is* this?" Edgar said, delighted.

He closed his hand around the top of the pouch and the rainbow light disappeared. It felt cool, as if he had never opened it.

Edgar opened it again and emptied the contents into his hand.

Once the items left the pouch they seemed to lose their potency. The ceiling no longer danced with stars. Instead, seven tiny chunks glowed softly, each a brilliant color: sapphire, ruby, amber, emerald, diamond, fire, and obsidian. A small scroll stuck out between two hunks. Edgar opened it and read:

CREATION STONES

A peculiar urge took hold of him. He went to the nearest dreary wall and swiped the emerald chunk across the cement, leaving a shimmering green slash. He studied it curiously.

"Creation Stones, huh?"

He selected fire orange and swiped it crossways. He made another streak—ruby red.

A diamond white arc.

A sapphire blue squiggle.

An amber yellow circle.

A hard angle in obsidian black.

He paused, chest beating. He felt so alive, so … empowered. He applied the blue again. His fingers moved faster, dancing, swaying, jumping like an orchestra conductor's hands. They were out of his control. Something inside him rushed out, and the brilliant creation stones channeled the energy out of him, through his hands, and onto the wall.

Swip-swap.

Slip-slash.

He struck the wall in a frenzy of nimble strokes, alternating colors without thinking. It was all so natural. He worked furiously through the sweat and heat. Titillating joy burned inside him.

When he was finished, he stood back. Suddenly overcome with exhaustion, he stared at the wall, dumbfounded, like waking from a dream in a half-alert daze, wondering when the dream had ended and reality began. He restored the creation stones to their pouch, stumbled back a few steps, and passed out.

He came to his senses moments later and from the floor gazed upon his creation. It gave off a soft candescence, as if a bright candle held over him. He had a pretty good idea what the mural depicted—he just wasn't sure how *he* had created it.

Something flashed in the corner of his eye—company. Edgar got to his feet and wearily turned around.

"Stewpot," he cried. "I thought you were an evil creature."

Edgar hugged him. Stewpot, unaccustomed to physical affection, grew stiff as a board. His wide moose eyes glanced anxiously about the room.

"Stewpot, look what I've done."

"Egger. Please."

"Isn't it great?" Edgar said. "I'm so glad it's you and not—"

Edgar stopped cold. Stewpot was *not* his only visitor.

The door swung casually open. Standing in the hallway outside was Uncle Warnock. His big arms were folded. Cream filling sat in the corners of his angry mouth. The light in the room was ample, spreading from the mural, but the shadows of the corridors seemed to reach out, swallowing Uncle Warnock, reluctant to part from him. He entered the room.

Edgar let go of Stewpot.

"Uncle, I…" He couldn't speak—there was a dry lump in his throat.

Warnock unfolded his arms and coolly took a pastry from his tunic.

"That's interesting," he said, observing the colorful wall. His voice was softer than it had ever been. Warnock bit down on the pastry, squirting cream down his chin. He licked it up carefully with his fat tongue. "What have you done, Boy?"

His sudden coolness worried Edgar.

"Huh? What have you got to say for yourself?"

Edgar looked uneasily at the wall, which brimmed with color. His uncle wore an arrogant smile.

"You have no idea, do you? Of course you haven't. Tell me, where did you get the paints? I will burn them immediately."

Edgar was silent. He'd rather die than give up his one possession.

"Makes no difference." Warnock paced around the room. "Funny," he said, "You really have no idea. You don't even know what it is you've painted. You're an idiot!" He coughed with laughter. "Well, this is what you want—fine. I'll no longer protect you from—" He glanced toward the door. "*From HIM,*" he whispered. "*Or* from the factory. You took your safe little life for granted. You *had* to sneak around. You *had* to venture out even when I, for your own good, forbade it. Always whining to your girlfriend Stewpot over there about there being … more than these walls, more than these doors. Well, I'm going to give you what you want, you little—" Warnock cut off. Smiling, he said, "You little *boy*. Have at the world—it's yours to explore. Stewpot?"

Stewpot stared dumbly at Warnock. "But, I don' want to."

"*Stew*pot," he repeated more forcefully.

Stewpot shuffled into the hallway and disappeared, his head sunk low. Warnock turned back to Edgar.

"Stop cowering. The door is open. You wanted out so badly, you can go out. I won't stop you. I don't care any more."

Edgar couldn't believe how phony his uncle sounded. He waited for the surprise blow. It never came. Warnock stopped in the doorway. "You dig your own grave, Boy."

He stuck his nose into the air, turned on his heels, and marched away.

Edgar was shocked. What *had* he painted? There was something familiar about the mural. He wasn't sure why—he just got the feeling it hadn't come from any book. This image felt much closer to him, like he'd seen it before. But he knew this to be impossible. The more he contemplated the image, the brighter the mural seemed to glow.

From the doorway, Edgar peered out into the corridor, expecting to see Warnock hiding outside, just aching to pop out and scream, "JUST KIDDING, MAGGOT!" But the hall was empty. Nothing unusual. Except, of course, that he was free.

Edgar knew not to waste an opportunity like this. He stepped out and moved quickly along. Instinct was guiding him.

When he was out of sight, a mysterious gust whooshed down the corridor, slamming his door shut. A figure wearing a cloak appeared magically, gazing from beneath a large hood. It appeared to stand guard outside Edgar's room.

But when it looked to the right and saw a shadow approaching, it quickly vanished through the nearest wall.

The shadow immediately fell over the spot where the cloaked figure had stood moments ago. The door to Edgar's room shook beneath the force of a heavy blow, but showed no signs of giving. The shadow hovered for a moment, then proceeded down the corridor, like a black cloud creeping.

The mural inside, an uncanny depiction of the factory, a gleaming scar amid a colorful sunset—quite dangerous anyone can see—immediately lost its luster, somehow aware that no one would ever gaze upon it again.

5

THE SHADOW AND THE TREMBLING ROOM

He felt it again. Something was following him. This was not the same feeling he got listening to the ghost voices of Marge McGinty or others like her. This was a creeping sensation in the pit of his stomach. And something else.

Edgar stopped in front of a shadowy enclave where the corridor came to a dead-end. It wasn't right. He knew these corridors, and the only way this dead-end could be here was if—

Edgar's stomach turned. The corridors had changed.

It made perfect sense now. How else had the wooden door gone unseen for years? Or the escape grate out of the grimy passage gone unnoticed? Something odd was afoot. He could no more trust the layout of the maze of halls than he could Warnock's recent nonchalance. Edgar checked the floor for threes. As long as he had those, he would find his way.

But there were no threes.

He noticed something else unusual—two yellow dots in the shadows of the dead-end. They hadn't been there a moment ago. Had they? Edgar stepped closer, peering into the dark. The dots suddenly moved, and Edgar felt the hair rise on his neck. They weren't dots—they were eyes.

There are things in this place that want you dead.

Edgar did the sensible thing. He turned and ran.

His mind was a flurry, the creepy feeling in his gut advising him to move as fast as he could. He bolted down a corridor to his left and pushed frantically against each door in a row of three. None budged. He rushed to a bend at the end of that corridor and wheeled around it. There were five doors in this one, and he found them all locked. He blindly navigated several more turns, stopping only once to avoid a dead-end. When he was certain he'd gotten far enough away, he checked over his shoulder. Utter disbelief.

Not far behind him, an ominous cloud of darkness drifted his way. The lights in the ceiling flickered out one by one. He didn't need to see the yellow eyes to know that the creature was hidden somewhere in that cloud.

Edgar darted off, picking up speed, frenzied, running so fast the walls and doors blurred by him.

He cut in and out of corridors trying to outrun the shadow, swung round bends and dashed the length of each straightaway, until finally a flash of hope. He turned into a corridor to his left, and was greeted by a sparkling arc of blue threes.

Edgar followed the trail like a dog hot on a scent (like Mitch the Mongrel in one of his favorite books *A Tail of Two Cities*) all the way around another turn, where it cut sharply into a door. Edgar didn't stop—he barreled into it, shoulder first. The door gave.

He lunged into the room, slammed the door closed, and fumbled with an entire battery of chain locks, securing three with frantic, clumsy fingers, before a massive force rammed the door, knocking him down.

Edgar stared at the door, praying. The creature outside banged against it again. The locks held. A little relief came over him—now he had to find another way out. He turned, and his heart sank.

The trail had led him to the bathroom.

One latrine hung from the wall by a rusty pipe. A lone toilet sat beside it. Once it might have been bright white porcelain. Now it was a pizzafied mess of dark green, brown, and purple. On the far wall, he spotted the outline of another door.

Someone had tiled in the doorway. He pushed hard on it but found it was as firm as stone.

The creature banged against the other door, knocking debris from the wall. The locks were holding, but they wouldn't last. Edgar spun around. Above the nasty old toilet, he saw a three floating in the air.

He grabbed at it, and pulled back in surprise. This three was made of ice.

The creature rammed the door three quick times in succession. The locks shook, their moorings loosening.

He looked at the three, the filthy toilet.

"There has to be another way," he moaned.

Another boom. One of the locks exploded off the door. No more waiting. Edgar sank his fingers into a half-inch of snotty grime and pushed the handle. It gave easily, the sound of a plunger and chain dangling without any water.

The creature wasn't letting up. It pounded the door until another lock gave way.

Edgar slapped the floating icy three in frustration, smashing it into pieces against the floor. What could he do? But then he noticed it: the outline of the door on the far wall had changed into a small passage. He dove through it as the final lock on the bathroom door broke free.

Edgar made it inside the passage. Behind him, the secret entrance closed without a sound, sealing him safely inside. He was not surprised to find a softly glowing blue wall where the door had been.

He thought, better not to wait and find out if yellow-eyed creatures could get into the tunnel as well, and moved on.

The passage transitioned into a polished tunnel the farther he went. The dirt floor and ceiling smoothed into cement. Soft light illuminated through long narrow slits. And strange copper plating adorned the walls at waist level. Edgar studied the plating thoughtfully, unsettled by it.

He'd read hundreds of books over the years thanks to Stewpot's uncanny ability to find them wherever he did.

He'd sacrificed hours of sleep for many a good story. Page by page, he'd gained a worldly bank of knowledge far surpassing the factory walls. Through his imagination, he traveled the universe; he summoned images both glorious and baffling. Even though Warnock eventually found each book and burned it to cinders, Edgar was able to get by on the assurance that Stewpot would soon bring him another.

But sometimes Edgar dreamed of things he had not read in books. He envisioned a stranger in a cloak, coming to take him. He tried to see the figure clearly, but could never get his mind around it. The figure darted out of view before he could get a good look. Another vision of a great Banyan tree with colorful leaves appeared to him when he felt really down. Most baffling, though, was the dream he had of a mammoth set of copper-plated globes, a machine of some sort. Not like the machines he occasionally glimpsed before a door slammed shut—this was grander, brighter, cleaner, more … powerful.

All three called to him. As different as the visions were, Edgar felt in his heart that they were linked.

He'd had the dream about the stranger in a cloak seven out of the last nine nights. Edgar hardly thought it coincidental given his uncle's recent mutterings. He'd overheard Warnock talking to himself about the cloaked stranger several times lately. Warnock seemed jumpier than usual, too. A year ago, the Crillow gag wouldn't have stood a chance. Warnock would've seen right through it and beaten both him and Stewpot to a pulp for a prank like that. But he'd panicked at the sound of slapping Crillow feet and squealed out of the room, two things Edgar had never seen his uncle do before.

Something funny was definitely going on in the factory. The last few days had proved that. What concerned him was the way he woke up feeling cold and empty. And the way the vision of the Banyan Tree came to soothe him recently to little effect.

Now the machine. Edgar tried to remember a time he'd seen anything remotely similar to the mammoth copper-plated globes from his dreams. There, in the tunnel, was the first. The metal plates running the length, though tarnished and old, showed signs of having once been brilliant and shiny. Had his pristine globes suffered a similar fate? Was it all somehow connected?

Edgar lost his train of thought to a deep grumbling

sound. It seemed to be coming from far below him. It got louder, working its way toward his feet. Without warning, the whole tunnel shook. The lights flickered. The walls rocked. And as quickly as it had come, the trembling passed.

Edgar stood for a moment dumbfounded. He questioned whether he'd just imagined that whole ordeal—he had gone without food after some time and was feeling a little faint. Speaking of that—he dug a bit of stone hard bread out of his trousers and ate the last of it.

With his hunger stalled, he walked for a long while without incident, until the walls of the passage tapered toward a tall rectangular doorway.

He stood in it looking into a long, narrow room. At the other end, the tunnel appeared to pick up again through a rectangular doorway exactly like this one. There was something eerie about the chamber. Its only light came from the tunnels on either end, adequate though increasingly diffuse approaching the center. The room looked about three feet wide, with walls stretching above to a shadowy point. Large stone slabs comprised the floor, which was littered with rubble and, worse, radiated heat. Edgar wiped oily sweat from his forehead and stepped into the room.

He got one foot in when another grumble came from below. The room rattled lightly. A soft roar filled the chamber, different from in the tunnel. Then, it came. An explosive force shook the room. Rocks toppled down, smashing into pieces. Rubble skittered across the floor. Intense heat breathed in. Edgar jumped back inside the tunnel right before a rock the size of his head bludgeoned him to death.

The rumble stopped. Bits of rock fell in afterthought. A plume of dust drifted toward Edgar, passed through him into the tunnel. He turned and watched it lose momentum and finally dissipate in the glow of the illuminated slits. Turning back to the room, Edgar had to rub his eyes, because the floor appeared to be moving.

But he wasn't imagining things. The slabs rose and fell in soft waves as though floating atop water. He watched the floor wobble for a few moments, then slowly reset. The slabs realigned, looking firm in their original position. Edgar decided to test them. Bracing himself in the doorway, he poked the nearest slab with his toe. A little more confident, he walked out onto them. They felt surprisingly solid.

He jumped on them several times, unable to budge them. The sensation of solid ground was assuring. He began the long walk through the room to the tunnel on the other side.

He got halfway across, where the light was dimmest, and paused. He thought he heard another grumble approaching. False alarm. He continued to make his way across the room. The walls felt narrower than before, the way he kept bumping into them.

The air was still—sweltering, but still. Ahead, where the tunnel resumed through the rectangular doorway on the other side, the long illuminated slits flickered. The farthest one went completely dark. Two lights nearer the chamber flickered out. One by one they all proceeded to blip out to darkness. Edgar didn't like the look of this. He squinted to see what was causing it. As the last few tunnel lights nearest the chamber flickered out, the path before him fell under a shadow.

Edgar glanced back. The tunnel he'd come from was full of light. So what was going on at this end?

Two yellow eyes emerged from the dark tunnel entrance, and Edgar felt a jolt of fear. The thing in the shadows! He turned and bolted back to the entrance, once again on the run from that thing. He ran with everything he had, his feet pounding the concrete. There was nowhere to hide, nowhere to turn. All of a sudden, the narrow walls felt suffocating. And the heat…

Edgar came into the light of the tunnel up ahead—it was strangely reassuring. Suddenly, he was taken by a horrifying detail. The light at his feet was diminishing. The shadowy cloud had caught up to him, and now it pressed in front, swallowing him in darkness. The slit lights in the tunnel ahead began to flicker. Edgar felt the creature on the back of his neck, breathing, and imagined its heinous arms opened wide to grab him.

Then—a misstep.

Time slowed but Edgar's senses were suddenly keener. His foot slipped and continued to slide outward. His ankle twisted as his legs stretched painfully apart. His palms scraped gravel. A heavy force connected with the back of his head, the blow bending him over.

The most horrifying thing he had ever seen floated past. It landed feet away, turned, and faced him.

Edgar knew the second it curled round—*IT*.

IT was the biggest wolf he'd ever imagined, four times

his size, fur as black as coal, two dangerous fangs protruding. Its amber eyes shimmered amid the darkness that engulfed it.

Edgar's heart beat heavily. The fall had saved his life, but the wolf blocked his way again. To get back to the secret bathroom passage, he'd have to go through IT. Not a possibility. But, behind him was a menacingly long straightaway in the narrow chamber. He could make a break for it, but IT would catch him before he got there. And then, even if he managed to outrun it, he didn't know where the tunnel on the other side lead. More mantises? A dead end? He bent his knee and pulled it back toward his body. At least nothing was broken.

The wolf's lips peeled back in a grin.

Can't be, Edgar thought. Wolves can't smile.

"*Yesssss*," it hissed.

"What do you want?" Edgar blurted, choked with fear.

A look of triumph spread across IT's long, powerful muzzle. Edgar found his voice.

"Get away. I know what you are!"

"Desssspicable boy," it said in a dark voice.

"Massssster's going to be very pleased to know you're finally dead."

"But I'm not dead..."

Its amber eyes flashed. Edgar tried to stall him.

"Wait! What master?"

"Ssstupid boy. There is only one massssster." IT reared back, rolling its massive shoulders forward beneath a spike of fur, and roared, "HIM!"

Edgar covered himself for the blow that would end his life. Waiting, he felt the stones pulse softly beneath him, a grumble rising. IT must have felt it, too, because Edgar was still alive. He opened his eyes. IT loomed above him, hesitant.

A concussion shook the room, sending the wolf onto its back, followed by a quake more powerful than the others combined.

Rocks showered down. Clouds of dust burst from the walls. The stone slabs wobbled and bounced. The room filled with intense heat. This was his chance. Before the wolf figured out what had happened, Edgar got to his feet and made a break for the exit. With a head start, maybe he could get to the other end of the chamber.

The heat felt suffocating, waves of it rising up between the slabs. Edgar skipped from stone to stone beneath a shower of rock and debris. A large chunk fell at his feet and broke into two. The rocking and swaying beneath him became too violent. Edgar braced himself between the narrow walls. An insufferable burst of heat singed his eyebrows, and he glimpsed a sliver of bright red-orange in the crevices between slabs. It wasn't water—the slabs floated atop molten lava. It explained the heat but did little to comfort him. Those twenty or so steps across the undulating, lava-floating slabs looked treacherous. Edgar glanced behind him.

"I don't believe it!" he cried.

A stone's throw away, atop a single slab, IT held on. The rocking and swaying pitched him violently, yet IT somehow remained afloat.

He caught the wolf's eyes—empty, save a brooding lust for darkness—and tried to look away. They drew him in, mocked his weakness. *Just a boy*, they seemed to say. *Hardly a match for someone as dark and powerful as the likes of me. If only you knew how much of a disgrace you are.*

The last declaration struck Edgar like a blow to the chest. Not just a look, not a notion—a voice inside him had spoken those words, had hissed those words (*dissssss-grace...*)—a voice that was not his.

"Get out of me!" Edgar screamed. "Get out of me, wolf!"

The yellow eyes glimmered in triumph, confirming Edgar's fear. The wolf—IT—had gotten inside him.

The room started to settle. The tipping, curling stones softened to a mild rolling. Edgar went for the next slab, his feet steady. Rocks continued to fall. He dodged them with nimble footing. If he survived the wolf until the next tremble, he knew he had a better chance on the other side of the room, away from stones and lava.

As he worked his way closer, he noticed a figure dressed in white standing ahead in the rectangular doorway. He felt a sharp pain in his stomach. It was the cloaked stranger, he knew, waiting to take him if IT did not first. The figure raised its arm and swung it down. A rock whizzed by Edgar's face, missing him by inches.

With IT on his heels, Edgar dared not slow. And yet ... he dodged another rock. The figure in white persisted. He launched a third and fourth rock. One grazed Edgar's ear, soliciting a quick whimper of surprise.

Edgar squinted through the heat, while dodging, working his way toward the exit and the white figure. Peril seemed inevitable. In any case, he'd take the cloaked stranger over IT any day.

"EGGER! Egger, hurry."

The figure called out—it was Stewpot! Suddenly, Edgar's face lit up. He sprinted for the exit, ignoring the barrage.

Meanwhile, Stewpot picked up a chunk the size of his fist, cocked it back, and launched it over Edgar's shoulder. Edgar glanced back in time to see IT, in pursuit, swat the stone easily to the side.

Stewpot followed it up with another one, and it hit the wolf square in the muzzle. IT let out a bone-chilling howl—more annoyed than hurt.

Edgar barreled toward Stewpot, ducking beside him at the last second, nearly tackling him—though Stewpot held firm to the ground, determined, two more rocks in queue. The wolf advanced on them, bounding at incredible speeds. Calm, unflinching, Stewpot backed Edgar through the rectangular doorway and into the tunnel. He followed with a few sure steps, then pulled a hidden lever on the tunnel wall.

A metal grate with pointy teeth descended, sealing off the chamber with the floating stones. IT slammed into it, angered.

"Come," Stewpot said.

The wolf glowered through the grate, locking gazes with Edgar.

"Egger, please."

IT thrashed wildly at the grate, but it might as well have been a solid wall. For all its strength, the wolf was trapped. IT paused suddenly. Its eyes flashed in annoyance. Edgar felt it, too. The floor began to vibrate beneath them.

"Insssolent brat!" the wolf roared, staring into his eyes, his heart, with rage. Edgar didn't flinch. It was his turn to grin.

The wolf went wild, rip-roaring against the walls, throwing its body at the grate. Edgar took Stewpot's hand, and they turned away. The first massive force hit, but they were well along the tunnel, safe from the perils of the trembling room. Edgar didn't look back.

6

A QUIETER PLACE

A gust blew through the empty maze of corridors on the factory's main level. A door lazed open. A couple doors slammed shut. A light bulb fizzled out.

Below the labyrinth, in a different tangle of passageways, Stewpot led Edgar through a tunnel lined with copper plating. He operated hidden switches opening grates, navigated a series of squat hallways where his hat rubbed a trail in the dusty ceiling, and hopped through a doorway with the door blown clear off its hinges. It lay on the floor covered in dust.

Edgar followed quietly. His legs shook uncontrollably, as if he were still in the trembling room. Part of him still was. The encounter with IT, with the stones and the lava, had pierced his core.

"Egger, follow close."

Stewpot pulled him into a wide open room with hundreds of snaking pipes for a ceiling. He gripped a red lever hanging down from one, and a burst of steam shot by Edgar's head.

"Careful," Stewpot warned, "Steam's high. Girders tense. Stinkin' gauges too old." He rapped his knuckle against a glass gauge filled with rusty powder. "Over here. Sit. Please, Egger."

Two crates were near the wall before a small stove. Edgar sat while Stewpot removed a kettle from the stove. He scooped the briny broth into two tin cups with a broken ladle. "Please eat."

The smell of the broth assaulted Edgar with all the voracity of a Grendel beast (a scary but memorable monster from one of last year's books). He slurped from the cup, forgetting his manners, and didn't stop until he'd turned the tin bottom up and licked out the final drops. A low whine filled the air—Stewpot jumped up and spun a large metal wheel round with two hands, releasing steam from a fatty red pipe.

"How's yer stew?"

Edgar saw that Stewpot hadn't touched his and felt a pinch guilty. "It was … good," he said. "Where are we?"

Stewpot looked worried. "Mustn't tell boss," he said. "Not supposed to talk to you."

"What do you mean you're not supposed to talk to me?"

Stewpot stared at him, letting the silence in.

"Stewpot?"

"If I told ya somethin', you promise you wouldn't tell?"

"Of course."

"Boss is worried. Been talkin' in his sleep about the cloak."

Edgar felt his body tighten up. "The cloaked stranger?"

"Shhhhh!" Stewpot shushed loudly. "He hasn't seen it, Egger. He knows about it, but he hasn't seen it."

Edgar was completely lost. "Who? Uncle Warnock? Hasn't seen what?"

Stewpot glanced about the room, paranoid. He spoke in a soft voice, "The factory—it's alive."

Edgar's look of confusion deepened.

"The walls … know. They listen 'a us. They watch us. But the thing." Stewpot took a deep breath. He looked like he was fighting back the horrible urge to flee. "IT. The wolf. Is different from the factory. IT doesn't belong here. Boss spoke of IT. He knew IT was coming. In his sleep he was sayin' the cloak wasn't goin a' be happy, either."

"Stewpot, what's going on?"

"You weren't supposed to be here, Egger. You was a little boy when they brought you here."

Edgar was off his seat. "Who, Stewpot—who brought me here?"

Stewpot swallowed hard, his eyes dark and innocent. "Was your mother, Egger."

"My … mother?" The words moved slowly.

"An' the factory, too. It brought you."

"How can a factory bring me to itself?"

"It's alive. Part of it is … very powerful. But powerful bad now. Not good. But IT is worse. If IT's master HIM finds out you're alive, it'll be bad, Egger. More bad than anything in the world. That's why IT was here. Boss was talkin' in his sleep, and somehow I think IT caught wind of it. Not even the factory can keep IT from hearing things."

Edgar saw the wolf's face in his mind, glaring at him, grinning as it picked his soul apart. "But Stewpot, IT died. You trapped it in the room."

"Maybe." Stewpot's voice trailed off, unconvinced. He filled Edgar's cup with broth. "Eat more. You have to go back to your room. Boss said no, but it's the only safe place. He's too worried about hisself to watch me anymore. You hide out there. I'll try to protect you from IT."

Edgar suddenly felt angry. "And the factory—will you protect me from it?" he snapped. "How about the cloaked stranger?"

Stewpot looked off to the side.

"Stewpot, I'm not going back there."

"But—"

"No, I won't. I can't do that. There's more to the world than this." A skinny pipe above them rattled loudly. Stewpot relieved the steam with a simple twist of a lever. Edgar continued, "I know what I painted back in my room—I'm not stupid. It was the factory, Stewpot, from the outside. I don't know how I did it. I'm not sure what it is I created all around it, but there's a whole world out there. I'm tired of being stuck here!"

Edgar was surprised at how loudly his last statement had come out. Without thinking, he'd tightened his shoulders passionately and balled his hands into fists. Stewpot was taken aback, but he eventually slumped forward again. He sighed and said through a long face, "I've run out've books, Egger."

Edgar studied him for a moment. "It's okay, Stewpot. There'll be more somewhere. I'll find them."

Stewpot gazed off, a bemused smile spreading across his face as he said dreamily, "Yeah…"

Edgar was ready to go. Despite the new information about IT and the factory being alive, he felt invigorated. He'd spent ages in his cell of a room, and he wasn't about to waste a second more. "Stewpot," he said, gently touching his shoulder. "You've been a good friend. Thank you for saving me back there. Thank you…" Edgar teared up. "Thank you for everything."

Stewpot watched Edgar head for the exit, but just as he got to the doorway, he blurted, "Was a sunset!"

Edgar stopped. "Beg your pardon?"

"Sunset's what you painted back there. Haven't seen it since I was a little boy, with me own parents. Was the mos' beautiful thing I ever saw. Thank *you* for that."

"You could come with me. We'll get out of here together."

"I belong here," he said sadly. "With these machines." He spun a little knob attached to a squiggly copper pipe, emitting one tiny steam puff. "Could'n leave 'em—they'd all rot."

"But Warnock could handle it. He's the Official Operator of Sludge and Machine Parts," Edgar said hopefully.

"Nah, Egger. He's jus' a bully, runnin' those m'chanical workers ragged with the sludge. The Machine—it's somethin' different. Good or bad, ye jus' learn to keep workin' on it. Hopin' fer a change again. And to stay outta the factory's way. You become part of it, and it forgets you, let's you carry on."

Edgar spotted a copper plate beneath him in the doorway and thought knowingly, *yeah, the machine.*

"Egger, say hi if you run into me mate while yer travelin'."

"There's another person here?"

"Dunno. Used to be, long ago."

"What's his name?"

"Maybe you can ask him for me."

Stewpot smiled as if he'd just made a great joke. Edgar dismissed it as usual Stewpot goofiness on par with balancing broomsticks. He smiled back before stepping out of the room and onto the flattened metal door, where a small set of footprints marked the dust beside a set of larger ones.

He quickly walked away without looking back. He pictured Stewpot's face, smiling—it was the happiest he'd ever seen him.

As he moved through the tunnels, Edgar wondered if his decision to leave Stewpot and go it alone was foolish. A gust whooshed past him, slamming doors in the distance. Stewpot's talk of the factory being alive didn't seem too far-fetched. And the business with IT and IT's master HIM—what did that all mean? What about mention of a friend, a mate? Things were much more complicated than he thought.

He felt burdened with exhaustion all of a sudden. Now that he'd appeased his hunger, it was hard to keep his eyes open. His thoughts a jumble of wonder and fatigue, Edgar stumbled a few more minutes before collapsing to the floor.

A fog closed in around him, light and airy, but he was already asleep.

7

STORAGE CLOSET B

Edgar dreamt of the machine shiny and new. Bright light gleamed off its copper plates. The mammoth spheres hummed with energy, clean vibrations emanating from its surface. A force lured him closer, the soft drone an irresistible lullaby. He gazed upon it, wanting more, but the dream was soon over.

The glorious vision left emptiness in its wake. Thoughts of creatures, dark and vast, villains and evil foes, passageways and chambers, strangers bearing warnings. Thoughts of freedom. Edgar sat up and opened his eyes. He'd ended up in a cramped room filled with oxygen masks and oxygen tanks.

He stood and puzzled over the stillness. The room looked as if it had not had a visitor in over a hundred years.

It looked … forgotten. Four oxygen tanks hung on the far wall, and two more lay on the ground. Dust blanketed everything in a green-brown sheen. Right beside the oxygen tanks, on hooks, were a handful of oxygen masks looking like the lifeless skins of giant flies. Edgar cringed; he was willing to bet those masks tasted *awfully* funny. He instinctively felt in his pocket for the velvet pouch, thinking with a smile, *this place sure could use some color*. He hesitated—better not. Better to wait until the time was right. He crossed over to the oxygen tanks and drew a line in the dust with his finger. After gathering a lung full, he blew a flurry of dust balls into the air.

"Oh," he whispered as one of the flurries landed right on the tip of his nose. Gathering another lung full, he gave a good burst in the direction of his nose. The dust ball didn't budge. It sat there, clinging to him for dear life.

He filled his chest a third time and, to be sure, he stuck his bottom lip out in position then forced all the air out in one quick, explosive blast—a force sure enough to remove even the clingiest of objects from his person.

But when he exhaled forcefully, a most unexpected

thing happened. A voice, tiny, but stout, yelled out, "Are you trying to kill me?!"

Edgar stumbled back into the wall, "Who's there?"

Once again, the voice, "I do say!"

Edgar glanced about the room, trying to pinpoint the location of the newcomer, but the room was small, and aside from the oxygen tanks and masks, there was no place to hide.

"I say, I say—stop flailing about like that!"

That voice was so near. Edgar felt a tiny prick and realized from where it came—he just couldn't believe it. He was definitely dreaming.

He leaned back and narrowed his gaze, his eyes going cross. There on the tip of his nose, barely in focus, sat a creature the size of a thimble.

"I say, are you trying to murder me?" the creature demanded to know.

"Wha-what are y-you?" Edgar stammered.

He was incredulous. "What am I? Are you blind?"

"No, I'm not blind. It's just … it's just…"

"It's just what?"

Edgar continued to stare.

"Stop staring, and give me your hand," it said. "Come on, put your hand up here. Careful! Not so fast. Nice and easy."

Edgar raised his hand to his nose, careful not to stir up a draft, and the creature stepped gingerly onto his index finger and wobbled onto his palm. It patted itself, as if brushing lint off its trousers.

"There," it said. "Much better."

Edgar was dumbfounded.

"Don't you know it isn't polite to stare?"

"I-I-don't…" Edgar didn't know what to say.

"Didn't your mother ever teach you not to stare?"

"My…mother?"

"Yes, your mother. Oh, I do say! Forget it. Just forget it. That's the problem with the world today—not enough mothers. And you—you *people*—are always trying to kill me."

Edgar had composed himself a little. "No, I didn't mean *that*."

"You don't just pick up a stranger and then try to *blow* him to kingdom come!"

"I didn't realize you were there."

"*I didn't realize you were there*," the creature repeated mockingly. "Then why did you blow three times? One time I can understand. Two times is careless. But three! Three times is plain mean."

"I don't want to be mean."

"Well, what did you expect, you big old—"

"HAROLD!" another strange voice boomed. The creature in Edgar's palm froze up instantly, and his tone of voice was entirely changed the next time he spoke.

"Margaret, I—"

"Don't you Margaret me! Get me down from here!"

The creature gave a shiver, and then addressed Edgar once more, its voice apologetic.

"If you don't mind, would you get my wife? She's in your hair."

"My hair!" Edgar exclaimed.

"Yes, she's right up there. If you lift me, I can get her."

Without thinking too much on this strange request, Edgar lifted his palm along with the tiny creature and held it above his ear, thinking he must surely look the fool right now.

A tiny grunt tickled his ear, and he felt the softest, lightest brush against his palm. The voice returned, "Got it. Everything is clear; you can lower us back down again. Easy, though!"

Edgar carefully brought his hand before his face. He expected to wake up at any moment or at the very least glance into his palm and see that there was nothing there and his mind was playing a trick on him. But either it was no trick or he had not yet awakened from this dream—there in the middle of his palm stood *two* tiny creatures.

Edgar narrowed his gaze, examining the creatures closely. His heart gave a little jump. "Are you … bunnies?"

"What does it look like, you big dumb—"

The new creature—the woman—quickly jabbed the first one in the stomach, cutting him off.

Edgar smiled. He couldn't believe what he was seeing. "You're dust bunnies!"

"Yes, dear, we're dust bunnies. And you mustn't pay any mind to my irritable husband. He doesn't mean to be so crass, but he's got a 'small man's' complex."

"Margaret!" the little dust bunny responded with distaste.

"DON'T you Margaret me!" his wife boomed. Then, in the sweetest voice, she addressed Edgar again, "Please excuse Harold. He's not as tough as he looks. Are you, dear?" Margaret patronizingly patted Harold's head. This seemed to infuriate him, but he didn't dare put in another word edgewise.

"Excuse me, Mr. and Mrs.…?"

"Just Margaret or Harold, dear."

"Mrs. Margaret, I am sorry to have bothered you and your husband."

"Oh, it's quite alright. Harold, isn't this boy a doll?" Harold, obviously still cross, uttered only a grunt. "It isn't every day we have visitors. Harold quite likes the peace. In fact, until yesterday, we hadn't had a visitor in twenty years. Imagine that—twenty years and no visitors. And that poor fellow long ago wouldn't have come if he hadn't been lost. Harold, what was his name?"

Harold raised both his dust paws in the air, "How should I know his name—it was twenty years ago!"

"Well, you get the point. Do pardon Harold's social skills; he doesn't have any."

"Wait," Edgar said. "You haven't had a visitor in twenty years?"

"That's correct."

Edgar looked confused. "But you said, 'until yesterday…'"

"So I did. That is, *almost* no visitors in twenty years ... excepting yesterday."

"Well, what happened yesterday?"

This time Harold: "Are you dense? She said we had a visitor."

"Harold!" Margaret reprimanded, her head shaking. Harold, having gotten away with more nastiness, folded his arms and gave a snort. Two dust bunny ears stood defiantly upright, and then flopped down. "Our visitor wasn't particularly nice to Harold. He said some things…" Margaret hesitated, carefully choosing her words. "He said some things that were a little threatening."

Edgar looked concerned. "Why on earth did he do that?"

"Good for nothing, that's why!"

"Harold, please. This young boy had nothing to do with that. Or did you?"

Four discerning dust bunny eyes studied Edgar. He found it hard to believe he was having a conversation with these little creatures, as they sat in the palm of his hand, no less, and he held them up to his face.

"Oh, I couldn't have had anything to do with that," he replied. Suddenly he thought of Stewpot alone in that room full of pipes, and realized he'd likely never see him again.

"Dear, is everything okay?" Margaret asked.

"I'm fine. Really."

"Margaret, don't you see the boy's upset? Why can't anybody leave anybody else alone? That's the problem with the world. No privacy. I remember when a bunny could have all the privacy he needed."

"Harold, please—put a lid on it. 'That's the problem with' this; 'that's the problem with' that! You're an expert on the problems of the world." Facing Edgar: "He is, too. He just doesn't do anything about solving them." Margaret shuffled a bit closer, coming to the base of Edgar's index finger. "Are you going to be okay, dear?"

Edgar sniffled, but when he did, Margaret was nearly sucked into the air. Luckily Harold grabbed her by the foot and held her back.

"Be careful, you oaf!"

"Harold, that isn't necessary. It isn't his fault he's so large and you're so small."

"I'm not small. I happen to be average height."

Margaret brought her paw to her face and mouthed the words, "Small man's complex."

Edgar smiled. He wasn't quite sure what it meant, but every time she said it, Harold got flustered, and this amused him.

"I'm sorry," Edgar said after a while. "I've had a really rough few days."

"Looks like it. Do tell us what's on your mind?"

"I was okay, I think, until a big dark wolf tried to murder me. I mean, that's not normal, is it?"

The dust bunnies were dead silent, their faces suddenly grave. Margaret's tone was completely different.

"Dear, did you say wolf?"

Harold, too, was a different bunny altogether. "Almost murdered by a big dark wolf?"

Edgar felt uncomfortably tense. "That's correct."

The two dust bunnies studied each other. Margaret turned to Edgar, took a deep breath, and began, "We've been in this place for a long time, and it didn't used to always be like this, you know. Used to be a fine place—not all this grime and darkness. Then *He* came along—or whatever they call him—and things changed. The darkness came. Soot and grime covered the place, making it difficult for our kind to move. Our brothers and sisters got stuck in the gooey surfaces. Our elderly kin fell ill. It wasn't long before Harold and I found ourselves alone."

Margaret paused, reflecting, great sadness in her voice. She continued: "Murder—used to be a word we used only to refer to a large number of crows. Then the Crillows—wretched creatures—chased *them* out. The air became filthy. Sludge replaced the rivers and tributaries around the island. Word got out that the sun had disappeared forever and that one day soon the light would fade away for good. We're dust bunnies; we can live without light, but there are plenty of species that cannot—plenty of good, honest, hard-working species.

"Used to be a splendid place. I'm afraid it's been like *this* for ages. We thought it would get better, that the factory was only going through a dark spell. Little did we know the spell was permanent. Been over a century in fact.

Imagine that—over a hundred years! But at least Harold and I have had each other. And we've been left alone for the most part. This used to be a busy room, you know. Doesn't look like much now, but this was the break area. Lots of workers in this place at one time—they used to take breaks outside, eat sandwiches and talk about 'Tha' lady'. Let the sun in for a while. Laugh.

"When the darkness came, the workers disappeared. There was a period of about ten years when we didn't see another soul. We thought maybe the light would return, that they were working on fixing the problem, but that was all misguided hope. Meanwhile, Harold and I kept to ourselves. We made a home out of the space. One day a new fleet of workers arrived—grim, covered in protective suits, silent. They placed locks on all the doors and filled the room with those large canisters and the strange face skins. They sprayed chemical in the doorways and nearly killed us with it. For a while, they used the room for their own purposes, wearing the face skins, putting the canisters on their backs, and venturing outside the factory. It was a disgrace to see how the place changed. Outside, you couldn't even see the sky. There used to be trees, you know—great big colorful trees all over the island. They're dead now—it's a cemetery of long gray tree husks and dark clouds.

"After a time, even the new workers started to diminish in number. They visited this room less frequently, and soon enough they stopped coming altogether. That was about fifty years ago. Nowadays, we hardly see a soul. It's as if the factory is a ghost town.

"But we hear things. Not often—only once or twice in a decade. But there are times when the nights are filled with howling, or the halls echo with a voice that turns my blood cold. It's a frightful thing that's happened, but Harold and I make do. There is nothing we can change. We're dust bunnies after all. Look at us—we cringe if you move too fast. It takes only a slight draft to send us tumbling.

"Yesterday, a very strange thing happened. You see, the whole factory's been going through changes ever since the darkness came, but not quite like this—not this fast. The changes that occurred before took years and years. But lately, the voices echo the halls much more frequently. Footsteps—or a sound like claws scratching—can be heard at all hours of the day and night. And yesterday, we had a visitor. Very strange. It was a new worker. A worker we had never seen before—and he was alone."

"What did he look like?" Edgar blurted. He could contain his curiosity no longer. This time Harold stepped forward to answer.

"Was a big fella," he said. "Big for your kind. With a belly that stuck out like he'd swallowed five or six of those big canisters whole."

"Warnock," Edgar gasped.

"You know him, then?"

"Yes," Edgar hesitated. "He's my uncle."

Harold shivered. "That's a wretched sort—said some things in mighty distaste."

"Dear, you don't have to say," Margaret assured her husband. She offered an explanation, "The big man came into this room frantic. You could tell he was a little disturbed…you know, in the head. He was talking to himself real loud, and he had difficulty breathing. His throat whistled between words, howling as he sucked in air. We hadn't had a visitor in so long he made footprints in the floor. See—over there."

Edgar directed his gaze toward the center of the floor, where he saw three wide and massive footprints in the dust.

"Disgusting," Harold blurted. "He had these doughy balls in his hands that he constantly bit from. Creamy stuff squirted across his fingers—and the way he licked it off!"

"Please, dear, we don't need all those details."

"Utterly disgusting."

"He seemed to be looking for something," Margaret continued. "He picked up one of the canisters over there, and he threw it across the room. Then, very strange, he picked it back up and leaned it against the wall where you see it now. Harold tried to stop him; this is our home you know!"

"I yelled right at that big dummy," Harold cut in. His face was twisted in anger. "I yelled for him to get his fat paws off our home and to leave us alone. Whatever he was looking for, we didn't have it. What possibly could he have wanted here? And you know what that fat weasel did?"

"Harold!"

"He bent down low, looked me right in my face, and laughed. He laughed at me." Recalling the incident made

Harold all tense with rage. He couldn't even finish his thought he was so perturbed. Margaret took the reins.

"The big fella called my husband a 'miniscule, dirty midget creature.' And you know about my husband's complex. Do not refer to his height—only I can do that."

Harold crossed his arms and huffed his disapproval.

"And when Harold went to punch that meany in the nose, the scary man puffed his cheeks and blew. My husband shot into the air. It was awful."

Harold pushed Margaret aside, his fists raised for effect, "It was the awfullest smell I have ever known—and that ogre didn't just blow out air, either. All that creamy white stuff he'd been stuffing into his gullet sprayed out when he blew. It was like a rain shower of goo. I'll be having nightmares about if for the rest of my life."

Edgar agreed that Warnock was disgusting. It was one he'd, too, never forget, the smell of sour milk mixed with that gunk found under one's toenail. Despite the seriousness of the story, the thought of Harold standing up to Warnock and getting blown into the air caused Edgar to smile. But he quickly fought it back.

"You mentioned that the man was talking to himself," Edgar said. "What was he saying?"

"Ah," Margaret said, raising her index finger high into the air. "You are right. He was saying some very strange things. Looking, looking, looking. He was like the March Hare—late for a very important date!"

"I'm afraid I don't understand what you mean," Edgar replied.

"We can't be sure what he was looking for, but he was definitely looking for something, the way he threw things about so carelessly. It was as if he expected to find something underneath the canisters, as if it had just fallen out of his pocket and rolled there. What he *said*, though, was most peculiar."

"What did he say?" Edgar was brimming with anxiousness.

"He was ranting about 'that wretched boy—that unfit vermin.'"

Edgar frowned. "He meant me."

Margaret paused, studying the boy along the tip of her nose. "So he did, so he did," she said. "Well, I don't see what all the fuss was about then. Certainly, he was preoccupied. After a moment, the man's face grew very dark. He had the look of someone who is in the worst kind of trouble and is working furiously to get himself out of it. But there was no getting out of it for this fella. The more he looked without finding whatever it was he was searching for, the more frustrated he became, and he began to speak gibberish. Kept saying—and I quote—'Got to hide. Got to hide. The cloak is coming for me.'"

"The cloaked stranger!" Edgar declared fearfully.

"Yes!" Margaret beamed. "Yes, that's right. And he occasionally blurted, 'If it doesn't get me, HIM will.'"

"HIM!" Edgar squealed.

"I know," Margaret agreed. "Deplorable grammar!"

"Grammar?"

"Yes, just deplorable. You know they don't teach grammar these days like they used to. We live in a society of degenerates and half-wits. That ogre said, 'If it doesn't get me, *HIM* will.' One should never use "him" when "him" refers to the object of a clause. No, one should say, 'If it doesn't get me, *he* will.' It's dreadful, really."

Edgar gave Margaret a blank stare. What on earth was she talking about? She seemed to let the point go, however, and her expression changed from studious to concerned. She whispered as if she did not want anyone save Edgar to hear her:

"I have heard of HIM, you know."

Edgar brought her closer, and he, too, whispered, "What have you heard?"

"Well, when you've been around a long time like Harold and I have, you hear things. Sometimes you hear strange noises or sounds. Sometimes you aren't sure what you're hearing, but you still hear something. Other times, whispers echo through the walls and corridors, carrying on a draft or lingering in the stillness of the night. We hear things. What you need to know, Young Man, is that He—or HIM or whatever they call him—is very dangerous…and not in any way that a scary wolf is. Just take my word for it: his kind of scariness is not physical, and that's the worst kind there is. A great deal of mystery surrounds this place, and He has much to do with that. Fear HIM more than you fear the darkness. And if it's He who you're after—or, worse, the other way around—then I am deeply sorry. That is all I am going to say."

Margaret stepped back on the palm beside Harold, and

Edgar studied them both. The stillness of the room, the silence—it was as if time had come to a halt. And Edgar was anxious. Margaret pulled her husband closer—he had been falling asleep on his feet—and said in a tone of closure, "Thank you for listening to an old dust bunny rant. We don't get fresh ears around here too often, as you know."

"Mrs. Margaret, please ... I have enjoyed our conversation."

A genuine smile lit up Margaret's face.

"By the way," she said. "Does our guest have a name?"

"*My* name?" Edgar felt foolish for clarifying, but no one had ever asked to know his name before.

Harold, finally alive, sputtered, "Are there *two* of you standing there? Of course, *your* name."

"Harold!" Margaret reprimanded—to no effect.

"My ... my name is Edgar."

Harold seemed surprised. "Did you say 'Edgar'?"

Margaret likewise: "Edgar! Edgar what?"

"Oh, well my full name is Edgar Trunk."

The two dust bunnies gave a resounding sigh of disappointment.

"What is it?" Edgar asked.

Margaret said quickly, "Oh, nothing."

Harold nudged her, clearing his throat derisively. Margaret explained, "It's just that there was talk some time back about a boy. A rumor had spread about a boy said to be descended from a long line of inventors."

"Inventors?"

Margaret looked displeased. "What *are* they teaching young boys these days? Well, it doesn't matter. You see, Young Man—Edgar Trunk—many years ago, and I mean over a century ago, a team of inventors built this place. Built the factory. Built the machine. Built everything. Oh, it was a sight, too." Thinking upon the days before the darkness had caused Margaret's shoulders to lift with fondness and nostalgia. Then, glancing once around the room, seeing the general decay and the looming shadows, her shoulders slumped back down, her face seeming to acknowledge, 'but those are the days of old.'

Edgar on the other hand came alive. "Who was this boy?" he implored. "Was his name Edgar, too?"

"Oh, yes, indeed, his name was Edgar."

"How long ago was it—exactly?"

"Harold?"

"Er, I dare say it was about ten years ago. Don't you think?"

"I think I wouldn't have asked you if I already knew the answer. Silly Harold."

As the two carried on in this way, Edgar wondered whether there *was* another boy in the factory who bore the same name as him. A boy descended from a long line of inventors responsible for building the factory when it was splendid and magnificent—imagine! He envisioned the place clean and happy, with workers who talked about "Tha' Lady" and ate sandwiches at lunchtime. Poor Mr. and Mrs. Harold—a whole thriving community of family members! Edgar could not imagine the two places were one and the same. Yet he did not dismiss Mrs. Margaret's vision of a cleaner, purer, happier place, for he dreamt of such a place on many occasions.

An inventor. It sounded grand—it sounded *important*. Mrs. Margaret said inventors built this colossal factory sparkling and new—not vile and disgusting the way it turned out. Inventors sounded good; they did not sound capable of creating a place like the one he knew. No, the inventors had nothing to do with that. It was just like Mrs.

Margaret had said: the Darkness came. HIM—or He—had brought the shadows and the curse upon these halls and rooms. It was HIM—who was scarier than the worst kind of evil, but in a way much worse than the physical. What *did* Mrs. Margaret mean by that? He wondered. Visions of IT came to him, and he shuddered to think of his encounter. How could a thing be worse than IT?

"Beg your pardon," Edgar said—the thought just occurred to him. "What was the boy's *last* name?"

"Oh, it hardly matters," Margaret said. She then gave a silly laugh, as if realizing the absurdity of an unlikely idea a moment too late. "We thought he might be you."

Harold snorted. "Answer the boy's question, old gal; you're always getting off the point. He wants to know the other Edgar's last name; I've forgotten it." Harold coughed into his paw and then quietly mused, "I'm sure it wasn't Trunk, though—dreadful sounding name, Trunk, like an old storage hamper, yes…"

Margaret ignored her husband's comments. She was too busy considering the question, nibbling her lip in thought. Finally, she recalled, "Yes, his name was Edgar, which is why we both thought that you might … well, you're not anyway … but it was Edgar Noone."

"Edgar Noone?" Edgar Trunk repeated.

"Yes," Margaret said. "Edgar Noone. Queer name isn't it?"

"I suppose so," Edgar's voice trailed off. He repeated the name in his head, 'Edgar Noone, Edgar Noone, Edgar Noone,' thinking he might recall some story or some vague reference that proved he, too, had heard of just such a boy. He could think of nothing, though.

"Anyway," Margaret announced. "You are not him. Clearly. But that doesn't mean we don't like you. You are an honest, sincere, and delightful young man. Besides, rumors are only rumors. I often find they are merely echoes of the truth. Nevertheless…" her voice trailed off, her thought not worth remembering in its entirety. She clapped her hands together, stirring Harold from another snooze, and said, "Young Edgar Trunk, how may we help you on your way?"

"I'm searching for a way out of here."

Harold burst into laughter—Margaret quickly shut him up.

"Dear," she said. "That is quite dangerous. No one has come or gone in ages."

"That isn't true," Edgar said. "There are deliveries. Pastries for uncle, ingredients for stew, that sort of thing."

"Well, you may be right, but I don't suspect you've actually seen these people making the deliveries?"

Edgar thought about it. "Not exactly. But Warnock picks up the packages at the front door."

"I see. And where is this front door you speak of?"

"It's … well, somewhere forbidden."

"I see." Margaret and Harold shared an empathetic glance. Margaret continued, "It sounds to me like you could be right. After all, you've heard of this cloaked person before, and we never have, despite our age."

"Despite *your* age," Harold cut in crossly. "I'm still a pup."

"Right, Harold. You're quite the pup with your bad knees and constant bathroom breaks during the night. Edgar, I'm sorry for the interruption, but I was just going to tell you that you ought to be wary of anything you see or hear in this place. Things are different than they used to be. But if it's out of here you want to go, you're in the right place. Although, I strongly suggest you take the other way out—the way you came in."

Quickly—too quickly for any of them to respond—a strange gust blew into the room and slammed the door shut. Margaret and Harold were swept into the air.

Edgar panicked. In the dim light of the room, two swirling dust bunnies were undetectable. Harold's stout voice rang out, ranting, "Deplorable, despicable, contemptible, loathsome, appalling draft!"

Edgar spotted a tiny dust-brown flurry encircling his nose—then a slightly larger one just inches away from it. There was no time to waste; he stuck out his fingers and plucked the two flurries out of the air in two pointed stabs.

This time Margaret cried out, "The ears! Heavens, watch the ears!"

Edgar relaxed his pinch a hair as he placed Margaret beside her husband.

"Oh, that was strange," Margaret coughed.

"Despicable," Harold grumbled.

"Are you two okay?" Edgar said, but a quick examination of the two bunnies revealed that, though tiny in size, they were hardy and tough in spirit.

They recovered soon enough—being dust bunnies, they were accustomed to particular hazards—but Margaret still had a disconcerting look on her face.

"I'm sorry," she said.

"About what?" Edgar inquired, baffled.

"Didn't you hear it?" She then motioned toward the door from which he had first entered the room. Edgar directed his gaze accordingly, but failed to see the problem.

"What exactly is wrong?" he asked.

Harold, too, strained to see the issue. "My eyes and ears aren't what they used to be, Margaret. Why don't you help us out?"

"It's the door," Margaret explained to Harold. "Don't you find it odd we were just discussing ways our young friend might go from here, and one of the ways closes instantly?"

"Was a draft that did it," he responded.

"Nevertheless," she said.

Edgar lifted his little finger. "We'll just open it back up."

"Go ahead," she urged. "Try the knob."

Edgar went to the door, careful to keep from moving too

fast and stirring up a draft. When he got there, he reached for the handle with his free hand but never quite made it.

"There *is* no handle," he called out.

"No handle?" Harold coughed. He was just as surprised.

"No handle," Margaret confirmed. "It was removed long ago when the locks were added. Access only—no exit."

"No exit?" Edgar fought back the urge to panic.

"Well," Margaret affirmed, "not through that door."

"That settles it!" Harold proclaimed. "You're getting your wish."

Edgar studied the room. There was little else than six oxygen tanks and a handful of masks. A funny triangle sign on one wall had faded to illegibility. Directly opposite the door that shut was an empty aluminum-shelving unit. Its shelves had rusted through, and the green paint had dulled to soft brown. Three hefty footprints left in the dust marked the floor. Edgar craned his neck a bit closer—there was a large arrow beside the footprints that he had not noticed before. Like the other painted signs and surfaces, this one had faded to almost nothing. When he studied it, though, it was undeniable.

"That's odd," Edgar said. "There's an arrow pointing toward the metal shelves."

Margaret raised an eyebrow. "You should know this wasn't always a storage closet."

"Duh!" Harold blurted.

Margaret turned to her husband—she was a woman of great patience—and took his paw in hers. "Dear, be nice. Our young friend is going to do what has not been done in a very long time. He's going to venture outside."

Now that it seemed a reality, Edgar's face twisted in worry and surprise. "I am?"

Margaret casually brought her paws together and stood resolute. "Yes," she said. "But first you're going to have to move that hideous set of shelves."

8

A PATHLESS WOOD

Outside, the factory was a horrible place. Edgar had come to know this from Stewpot and from his uncle. Because of the immense pollution, only the Crillow stood a chance against the awful fumes.

Edgar had never seen a Crillow in real life, either, but he'd heard his uncle ranting about them in the halls. One particular detail resonated with him. Other than the gross physical deformities, his uncle referred on several occasions to the Crillow's sharp, penetrating scream, a thing he likened to the death wail of a wraith. A wraith was one thing Edgar had failed to come across in his vast reading. However, he did not really need to know what a wraith was, so long as he could imagine that its death wail was likely not a very pleasant sound. For one, a wail is a horrid sort of cry; it is a sound made by unhappy spirits. Second, any phrase with death in it is an unpleasant one (despite one narrator's view in the longwinded epic *The Happiest Death Ever*). Therefore, when one took two words, which separately were most awful, and combined them, the result was something best to avoid. This applied to wraiths, as well; should he ever meet one—and know what it was—he would turn the other way and run like mad. Or, should he ever hear that a wraith was coming to visit, Edgar would be sure to make himself unavailable during that wraith's stay. A little planning never hurt anyone.

Edgar considered the topic of planning as he wrapped his wits around exiting the factory into the toxic air. Fortunately, there were six oxygen tanks in the room—two of which were full—and a handful of oxygen masks. His uncle's burdensome drill had come in handy, after all. He donned the tank, but before sliding the mask over his face, he thanked Mrs. Margaret and Mr. Harold for their hospitality. They had been great company in the last hour, and he would miss them. Harold was just glad to have the rusty shelves moved to a different wall—good to change things up every 100 years or so, to keep things fresh.

Margaret and Harold waved from an ankle-high perch in the corner. They looked a mile away they were so small. Mrs. Margaret had informed Edgar of a smaller, narrower room between the storage closet and the outside—it had been implemented years ago to keep the toxic air from entering the factory. He entered it now, closing the door behind him and sealing the dust bunnies safely inside.

"This is it," he said. Edgar put his hand against the push-bar on the exit door and paused. As the expression goes, butterflies danced in his stomach (even though butterflies do not have dancing legs), which just means the levity of his situation washed over him: he was about to go where no boy had ever gone before.

Without another thought, he pushed the exit bar.

The door hardly budged at first; dry paint had gummed up the jambs. Another good shove loosened the crevices, and it released with ease. Edgar felt a burst of warm outside air. He then savored his first taste of stale oxygen, for he had been holding his breath in anticipation.

He stepped outside and gasped at the scene before him. A dismal world sick with gray. The earth was ashen and powdery. Foggy wisps drifted like lost souls among an endless wood of branchless tree trunks. The trunks, pale and malnourished, stretched above into a thick layer of smog. It hung down, an impenetrable ceiling of black that, the closer Edgar looked, revealed a slight oozing movement. No light could ever hope to penetrate the dark layer. And the treetops, engulfed by it, must have been a horrid sight.

Edgar stepped forward among the pale trunks. He pursued a general line formed by a row of them; there were no identifiable paths. He stopped when he was fully surrounded by the bleak setting and frowned. He wondered, *Whatever will become of this place*? His instincts told him the "whatever" had already become—all hope for change was gone. But did he really believe that? A thin wisp drifted toward him and passed over his mask in a silent cool breath. Oxygen, Edgar reminded himself, expires. Already his tank was feeling lighter (or was it heavier?).

Another drifting bit of fog passed through him like a ghost. Edgar studied his trail in the cracked, dry ground, and was comforted. If not for his footprints, he would be lost. Everything looked the same. The low smog ceiling gave the factory grounds the look of a room devoid of walls. Even outside the place was a labyrinth. He noticed a set of tracks other than his and knelt down for a better look.

He blinked, disbelieving. The tracks in the clay were fresh, shaped like human feet—bare feet with five distinguishable toes. Edgar glanced at his boots, and it hit him.

"Crillows!"

He didn't have to see them to know they were Crillows. Only they could survive the air. The grounds appeared empty. Wings fluttered in the distance.

He suddenly felt naked in the open, standing beside the tracks. There was nowhere to hide. Should a Crillow descend upon him from above he would be at its mercy. What he feared most of all was the death wail he'd been warned about. Who knew what one good wail would do to him?

Another flutter—this time louder, closer.

"Who's there?" Edgar whispered.

He stepped toward the nearest tree trunk and hooked his arm around it. The bark sloughed away beneath his touch. Edgar unhooked his arm at once, a broad indentation left in its place. He shivered. The sloughed bark and skin revealed the black core hidden beneath, which resembled a sick evil bone. Not long into his sojourn, he longed to be back in the halls. He moved on, searching the grounds. A worrisome feeling crawled through him. What was he doing out here? What *really* was he doing?

He picked up the pace in order to cover more ground, faster, slowing only to avoid bumping into two trees standing close together. He hoped to identify something of interest—*some*thing different out in the pathless wood. For all his fast-walking, the scenery remained constant, unchanging. If not for his trail of footprints wagging behind him, he would have thought himself lost.

Edgar knew something wasn't right. If this were truly an island, he thought, its grounds proved vast, even though he'd always known the river of sludge to be visible from the outside walls. Warnock claimed to have seen it on several occasions, threatening to toss Edgar in just to watch him do a dozen laps, a thing he announced with great melodrama, insisting the short walk to the banks would be nothing considering the chance to see a terrible brat get his comeuppance.

Edgar stopped farther ahead. He'd traveled a good distance, and there were no signs of the river.

He was taken by a wrenching feeling in his stomach.

So this, he thought, is how Captain Dan Tambers felt his first time at sea—isolated, alone on a small boat, surrounded by ocean on all sides, nothing in the distance but more distance. Edgar recalled a verse from Captain Tambers's book *Hope Floats, But a Mighty Heart Sinks*:

> *A thingum much liken a whale passed 'neath us. It had teeth on its head which went round its powerfulsome maw. The firs' mate pitched bread into the waters, 'long with all our meats 'n poultry stores. A hen was named Vespers—gallant farmy rogue that ha' lived with us fer months at sea, an' had made the waters his own, like a wolf 'at takes a likin' ta a kitten 'n raises it on 'er milk—he went in, too! We was payin' terrible homage to 'is beastly whale, fer 'im ta leave us be. But was the skipper who pointed out that what we was concerned as the sea's mos' terrifyin' minion was jus' a shadow caused by a cloud floatin' pas' the moon. An' he was right! An' all the rest of four days we was downright sad for Vespers.*

He was surrounded by an endless wood. A thick black ceiling pressed toward him from above, and, below, light wisps drifted like unsettled specters among the pale tree necks, ghosts of unhappy souls forever left wandering without hope. Edgar understood the feeling of Captain Dan Tambers and his crew on that night, the queasy sensation of stumbling into a haunting eternity.

He squatted down to rest the heavy oxygen tank and glanced casually into the distance. He'd covered a lot of ground—so much that he could no longer see the factory anywhere. At least he'd be able to find his way back by following—

His face went gray. "Impossible," he croaked. His trail of footprints had disappeared.

Edgar stood and spun around—surely this funny tasting oxygen was getting to his head—but as he searched the dry, cracked earth for his trail, reality sank in: both his head and his eyes were in working order. He was alone, lost in the pathless wood, and his oxygen was running out.

A spectral cirrus wisp lazed around him, blocking his view. He searched the ground in vain, fanning the fog so he could see. But when the wisp moved on, floating off among the distant tree husks, Edgar forgot about footprints in the dirt.

He had company.

Ten trunks beyond the edge of a row of trees sat a big fat Crillow.

Edgar's mind raced with dark and horrible images. Stories were one thing—*this* was real. He didn't dare move a muscle, not a single involuntary eyelid twitch. Still. Dead still.

The Crillow, too, sat frozen, as if it had entered into a staring contest with the nearest tree. Edgar was like a statue.

Did it see him? Did the awful creature even notice him standing there in horror? Eventually, one of them was going to have to move. But the bird-thing remained equally frozen. Its long wings formed small arches beside its body. It's feet—oh, goodness, its feet!—looked hideous. Edgar was close enough to see the toenails barely hanging on. A ghastly sight! It was as if they would just fall right off if caught on a stone or a root.

Edgar's only consoling thought was that the Crillow faced away from him. His muscles remained taut and unmoving. After all this time, the creature had not budged, and he wondered if it was even real.

A thin cirrus wisp enshrouded Edgar. His eyes fell upon the wisp instead of the horrible bird creature. He was hidden for a moment and allowed himself a giant breath. When the wisp promptly moved on, Edgar faced a maddening predicament: one Crillow now was two.

A pair of bird-things crouched only feet away. There was that word again—feet!—this time Edgar lost his focus to a full, uncontrolled body shiver.

The Crillows did not respond.

Precisely what was happening? He wondered feverishly. The thought struck him: what should happen if they both turned suddenly to see him and gave a resounding, echoing, gargantuan death wail? Edgar's imagination allowed him a glimpse into the future. His skin peeled back from his body. His bones obliterated to dust—a gruesome end to an unsatisfactory tale. And yet…

Those horrid aberrations did not move. Another wisp came and went, and a third Crillow appeared. It was as if the pale fog harvested the wretched things, depositing them at will wherever it liked.

Another wisp—another Crillow.

Now four Crillows sitting in a group. He had yet to see them move—not one feather, not one toe. Their wings bent beside their bodies pointed downward. Their beaks all faced ahead, away from Edgar. Their eyes, beady and dark, hid amid a swath of shiny black feathers, and while he could see their awful toes with sick clarity, he could not make out those eyes.

Edgar couldn't bear to see them multiply like that. Another wisp approached—he could just *feel* it. There would be five of the wretched things before long. Squeamishness won over him. Edgar slid one foot back, then the other, retreating.

He kept his eyes on the Crillows as he reached back with his hands to guide him. His fingers found the petrified skins of trees and effortlessly knocked hunks of flesh to the ground. The feeling sickened him, as if he were plunging his hands into moist pits full of cockroaches and earthworms. He didn't dare turn his back to those things, though. Another wisp passed through him, its cool touch chilling him to the bone, and sure enough a fifth Crillow was revealed among the others when it passed—lifeless, with crooked wings and pointing beak.

Edgar made his way backwards through the wood, growing bolder with time. When after fifty feet the bird creatures still showed no signs of life he picked up his pace, becoming careless, backing forcefully into narrow tree trunks, making a clatter. He passed beyond an inordinately large tree trunk and stepped behind it.

It was the first time he had taken his eyes off the Crillows, and he closed them in relief. He took deep breaths in an effort to calm his racing heart.

Something moved beside him. Edgar turned, catching the tail end of a feather moving out of sight.

"Who's there?" he muttered.

"Must you do that?" a voice called back from out of view. "They aren't dead, you know."

"What do you want?" Edgar backed into another tree.

"Do stop," the voice replied. "He didn't do anything to you."

"What are you talking about?"

"Look there—you see."

Edgar spun around and saw that he had gouged a hole in the wide tree trunk with his oxygen tank, exposing the shiny black core. He studied it cautiously. The sloughed-away bark and skin formed a pile on the ground. Inside, the slick black core glistened.

"They are alive."

Without looking up, he replied, "It's hideous." He

wasn't sure if the tree still lived, but if it did, it had become an aberration—not quite tree, not quite dead or alive, a gross creation of the island destroyed beyond any semblance of its original self.

"You're right about that."

Edgar admitted, "I've never seen trees like these."

"Not quite the same as your pretty Banyan, eh? Have to go a long way to find one of those."

Edgar suddenly looked up—he couldn't see anyone. "What do you know about that?"

"I know you dream of it. I know you were born beneath the branches of one in Fall, when the leaves were rust and brown and orange."

There was silence. Edgar's eyes fell upon the scar in the wide tree, but he did not see it any more. Instead, his thoughts occupied his gaze, projecting images before him, his great big Banyan tree. Wide-stretching knobby roots gripped the earth like ancient hands resting beneath a magnificent canopy of burnt orange leaves. A breeze rustled the leaves and branches, creating a shower of orange and brown flakes. *Was I born here?* he thought. The tree flickered out of view, and its glorious vision dissolved to a moist black gouge and a pile of dead skin.

"What do you know about my dreams?" Edgar asked solemnly.

"I know you want more than this from the world."

Edgar turned his ear toward the voice. "I know you," he said. "You saved me that day in the tunnel."

There was a brisk shuffle—the newcomer skirted farther into his hiding place.

"Don't worry," Edgar said. "I won't try to look at you. I know you don't like people seeing you."

"It's not that."

"Well, what then?"

Another shuffle. "If you saw me, Young Sir, you would be frightened."

"That's nonsense," Edgar replied. "I've seen plenty of frightening things, and none had a voice like yours."

"Young Sir?"

"There's kindness in it. It touches me. I don't know why, but it touches me."

"But if you saw me…"

"I won't see you," Edgar said, but as the words left his

mouth, the newcomer stepped into view, humbled, afraid, unable to look him in the face. Edgar whispered with only a hint of surprise, "*You ... you're a Crillow*."

The stranger stood trembling, his gaze directed sharply to the side. He had two ghastly old woman feet, which he hid behind his tail feathers, and his tiny beak bent down in a lasting grimace.

"I'm not afraid of you," Edgar said.

"You are," the creature whimpered. "I hear it in your voice."

Edgar gulped some oxygen. "Maybe a little. To be honest, I've never seen a Crillow before."

"We aren't awful, you know. We're good creatures—gentle, quiet."

"But the death wail," Edgar blurted.

"Oh, the death wail," the stranger moaned. "It's such a bad rap!"

"It's true then?"

"Young Sir, I've cackled a few tunes in my younger days that some would swear was a death wail, but nothing so awful as the stories that get told."

Edgar shifted his weight from one foot to the other. The stranger, either out of habit or out of courtesy, did the same.

"What did you mean earlier?"

"I don't know," the Crillow replied, shuffling his feet, examining the ground with the utmost concentration.

"These trees: did you mean to say that they are alive."

"Oh, that," he responded. "Yes. And no."

Edgar looked perplexed, and although the stranger did not dare glance in his direction, he added:

"You see, the trees as you call them aren't trees at all."

"They aren't?"

"Well, of course they *look* like trees, but looks cannot be trusted here."

"So I've heard. What are they, then?"

"What are they?" the Crillow was incredulous. "Why, they're people, of course."

"People?" Edgar backed away from the pile of bark skin—repulsed.

"Yes."

"Well, that's just awful that they've become trees."

"Don't feel too bad for them; they aren't *good* people… but they are people nonetheless."

"Nobody deserves this," Edgar cried.

"Why?" the stranger asked. "Do you know them?"

"No, I don't. It's just … I don't know what."

"Only natural, I suppose," the Crillow said. "Just trust me; if you had known these people before, you would not feel sorry for them. *They* put the big fella to shame."

"The big fella? Do you mean my Uncle Warnock?"

"Aye, him—terrible sort."

"I guess I kind of know what you mean." Edgar knelt down, and the bottom of his oxygen tank rested on the ground. "Now that's a load off," he said.

"Lodov," the Crillow replied. "Don't know him."

Edgar looked confused. When the stranger appeared to drop the issue, Edgar asked, "By the way, what's your name?"

"*My* name?" The Crillow turned suddenly and faced him for the first time. His eyes shone with sadness and surprise.

"Yes."

The creature was skeptical. "You want to know *my* name?"

"Yes, I do."

"Well, I … it's Sebastian."

Edgar tried it out, "Se-bas-tian … Sebastian." The Crillow looked sharply away again. "Sebastian, why are you so bashful?"

Sebastian's beak got a bit rosy. He shifted uncomfortably in place, thinking of how to respond. But the color left him instantly as he stood upright, pointing his beak into the distance. "No," he whispered. "Oh, no … please."

"What is it?" Edgar urged. "What do you see?"

"The fog, the fog," he said. "Come, hurry, we have to get moving."

Edgar looked up and saw one of the strange cirrus wisps approaching. "The fog? What's the matter with the fog?"

"Hurry, please! Come!" Sebastian skirted back away from him, skipping, trembling, his beak a curve of worry.

"But—"

Sebastian shuffled off, half flying, half skipping. Edgar chased after him, remembering their narrow escape from the mantises.

Sebastian navigated the wood with a keen sense of direction. He dodged the frequent tree trunks with ease, using his crooked wings for balance. Edgar struggled to keep up.

"Where are we going?"

"Almost there," Sebastian snapped. "Quick, do hurry."

He wondered where they were headed. The territory stretched on flat and endless. If they were going to escape, he guessed they were either going up or going down—certainly, up was not an option. The fog arced toward them, slow but persistent. Edgar had seen the fog place five Crillows on the ground, each frozen eerily in time. He wasn't sure what it all meant, but he knew by the queer feeling in his gut that something awful had befallen this place, something Sebastian fled with all the fear and passion he could muster.

"There!" Sebastian shouted finally. "There—quick. You'll have to take off your tank."

He stopped. Huffing for air, Edgar caught up to him, confirming his predictions: there was a dark hole at Sebastian's feet.

"Take off my tank—are you crazy?"

"Please," he said, "we don't have much time. Take off your tank—it's not *too* deep."

Sebastian, not wasting any time, hopped into the hole.

Edgar stooped over it and saw two shiny eyes wide with

fear, beckoning. He looked back at the wisp, which closed in on a bunch of tree trunks some twenty feet away. Now the hole again. Sebastian was right; for Edgar to fit down there, he would have to remove his oxygen tank. Of course, he could not breathe without it—he wasn't a Crillow.

"Sebastian, I just can't," Edgar said calmly. "Go on."

"But the fog!" he cried.

"No, really," Edgar said. "I'll be okay."

Edgar glanced at the airy wisp, now fifteen feet away and approaching lazily.

"Young Sir," the tiny voice pleaded from the hole. "You can breathe here—breathe real easy."

"Sebastian, I—"

Suddenly a loud clanging filled the air.

Edgar looked back, the sound rang out, a noise only large, heavy machine parts made. The light and easy fog was the only thing in sight.

Sebastian's voice trembled, "We've made it angry!"

"Made *what* angry? All I see is…"

The clanging hammered again. Edgar stared in disbelief—was it really coming from the fog?

"Come—breathe here. The factory. Let's go inside."

An overwhelming desire to *get out* came over him. He looked at the hole, at the fog again—the clanging pounded his head. Now he was frantic, too.

Edgar squatted down, peered into the hole, and saw two gesturing eyes. He sucked in one good lungful of funny tasting air, wriggled out of the oxygen tank straps, and dropped into the hole.

9

FALL FROM GRACE

With a snap, the air hose connecting the tank tore away, and Edgar landed on soft earth. He continued to hold his breath, resisting the welling pressure in his lungs, and pulled free of the mask. A blast of cool open air assaulted him. The fog hovered over the hole, clanging.

Sebastian pulled him into a dark tunnel, heaving with all his Crillow might, two old feet holding steady to the ground.

Edgar held his breath. He was in shock. He had gone from the seemingly dismal and eternal factory grounds to the grimy insides of the factory's infinite tunnels. The terrible clanging faded. His eyes adjusted.

Sebastian's tiny beak materialized inches from Edgar's nose. He cried out, releasing the funny-tasting oxygen from his lungs before gasping forcefully, drawing in what he hoped was breathable.

As Edgar waited for the toxic pollution of the island to enter his body and kill him, Sebastian cocked his head to the side, perplexed, wondering why in heavens he was making a face like *that*. Finally, he said dryly, "Are you all right?"

Edgar's senses had yet to catch up to him. He sputtered one long meaningless slew of words, "Wha- air breathe clanging fog weird Crillows frozen hammering sweaty funny tasting heavy tanks tunnel grime mantises…"

Then it was quiet. Edgar had run out of air. His body clearly understood that it could breathe; his mind just took a little longer. He was a mess—but he was alive.

"Now," Sebastian said. "All better?"

Edgar regained control of his faculties. "Please," he said. "Get me out of this tunnel."

"Oh, I know quite what you mean," Sebastian replied. He stepped away from Edgar and skipped a few paces down. He looked back with gleaming eyes. "Young Sir, not much farther—we're almost there."

Somehow, Edgar doubted this.

****

They traveled to a well-lit empty room at the end of a winding tunnel. Sebastian found a patch of shadow in a corner, trying to hide himself out of habit, unsuccessful in his attempts.

"I have a confession to make," Edgar said.

Sebastian looked up.

"Right before we met each other again, I had been trying to escape some Crillows. I'm sorry, but everything I had ever heard about your k—," a hesitation then, "*others* like you had been awful. Death wail and all." Edgar did not mention feet.

Sebastian cast his gaze to the side and frowned. He shuffled back and forth.

"I saw Crillows in the woods," Edgar continued. "The fog seemed to put them there. They just stood with their crooked wings like they wanted to move and couldn't. I got scared. I didn't know what was happening. I ran."

Sebastian's head twitched, his eyes darted side to side, as though reliving something horrible. He came together suddenly. He brought his frowning beak level with Edgar. He was focused.

"I am the last one," he began.

"Sebastian?"

"Many years ago, there was a change. The Darkness came. It blotted out the sun and stars. It made everything black and gray. Used to be a beautiful field out there, with green grass and wildflowers. We had butterflies. Now it's all trees. The evil ones took root—their plans backfiring. I think they underestimated IT—underestimated *HIM*. They thought they could tame it; make it work for them—make *IT* and make *HIM* work for them. They were wrong.

"We weren't always like this, you know. Crillows, I mean—with these ghastly feet. My *kind*, as you call us, were once sharp and cunning. We weren't *like* crows; we *were* crows. (Well, ravens, if you want to be PC about it all.) The Darkness, the imposters, and the pollution the factory began to pump into the air—it had a powerful effect on us. It forced our wings crooked. It turned our beautiful and dynamic talons into these wretched monstrosities."

Sebastian reflected for a moment. His shoulders drooped and his eyes watered.

"We learned to survive the new climate, when none of the other creatures could. We became outcasts—cursed things. Some of us never got over our transformations, never learned to live with them, and over time a great divide formed among our kind. We split into two factions: the Underlings and the Overlings. The Underlings retreated into the ground, made tunnels and linked them to the intricate network of the factory's. The Overlings took flight—only those of us strong enough to fly—and chose a life above the smog. It was rumored that, if one flew high enough, he could see the sun and stars. Those were only rumors, though. No Overling to take flight ever returned to associate with the ground-dwelling Underlings. That's what I am now—a ground dweller. I don't do well up there. These wings won't fly.

"We lived like that for a long time, split into two groups, living our own lives and keeping clear of each other. But a strange thing happened. The smog thickened, went from gray to black, and day by day it pressed toward the ground until it covered the leaves and branches of the forsaken—those horrid souls who got more than they had planned. And soon after, the spirit fog arrived. It was light and mobile—more a wisp than a fog—and it had magical powers. It had terrible powers. Suddenly and mysteriously the Underlings began to fall sick in the tunnels. Days after, when our number had been reduced to a handful, the Overlings returned. They began to fall from the sky—their wings broken and their beaks stiff. It was awful!

"Those Crillows you saw—the others—weren't really Crillows. Not really. Sure, they used to be, but what good's a body without a brain? Without a soul? It takes them. The fog takes them—most unwillingly, and some unknowingly—and it returns them just like you saw them. They come back empty. It makes me toss and turn at night. I don't sleep, Mr. Edgar. I haven't slept in a very long time. I wonder when it'll get me and put an end to the whole race."

Sebastian skipped over to the other corner and knelt there. Edgar, who did not want to seem insensitive, allowed him a few moments to reflect. But a thousand questions filled his head.

"What is it about the fog, Sebastian? How does it do such things?"

"Oh, that's a grave matter," he replied. "One I needn't explore with you, Young Sir, if you'll forgive me. There are things best left alone in this place, and the answer to that mystery is one of them. I suppose you'll ask about the alarm, though—that awful hammering sound that chased us down the hole."

Edgar nodded.

"All I know, it's not quite all fog. There's machine parts in there." Sebastian stood tall and hopped toward him. "Now," he said in a different tone. "That's enough on the topic of the fog."

Edgar wasn't satisfied. "Sebastian, wait," he interjected. "When you say machine parts, do you mean *factory* machine parts?"

Sebastian looked away. Edgar thought he was going to let his question trail off into the distance unanswered. But he turned to Edgar with a face full of sorrow and fear. "Do you know what you're asking?"

Edgar swallowed.

"Do you *really* know what you're asking?"

Edgar met Sebastian's serious gaze with one of equal weight. But Sebastian turned his head once more, and this time he actually cracked a sly little grin.

"I admit, I was skeptical about you at first," he said. "I didn't have all that much faith. I mean, a rumor's a rumor after all. But look at you. Look. At. *You*."

"Sebastian," Edgar said worriedly, "My name isn't Trunk, is it?"

The bird was silent once again. His face bore a shade of disbelief. "Yes and no," he said.

"My real name—it's Noone."

"Again, yes and no."

"Sebastian, are my parents inventors?"

"Yes."

"And I am descended from a long line of inventors?"

"Yes."

"Sebastian," Edgar said. "Sebastian…"

But Sebastian had disappeared.

Edgar glanced about the room and saw no traces of him.

"Sebastian," he called out.

No sign of his friend.

"That's just swell."

Edgar felt a stirring inside him, a feeling similar to the time he first discovered the trail of blue threes, and while he did not fully understand it, he did only what felt most natural to him: he stood up and walked over to the spot where Sebastian had stood, and he stared into the darkest corner of the room, waiting patiently, searching.

At first, nothing happened. No magical door appeared. No fairy arrived in a poof of yellow smoke. But as he lowered his head a touch, a shimmer caught his eye. It was the handle of a trapdoor.

Careful not to lose sight of it, Edgar moved just as slowly as he had when Mr. Harold and Mrs. Margaret had made his hand their perch, when the slightest draft threatened to send them airborne. He inched forward and rested his left knee in the dirt. He reached toward the handle and grabbed it. It was ice cold. He pulled, easily lifting the trapdoor, and slipped inside.

Edgar moved down the tunnel, weighing the gravity of Sebastian's words. "I am the last," he had said. The fog, or the Darkness, had changed his kind, had made them monstrous, and eventually a force of unknown origin wiped out his kin, leaving only him to scavenge the dismal grounds, leaving only him to flee the airy gray wisps and seek refuge in the tunnels beneath the factory. "What good's a body without a brain?" Sebastian had asked. And Edgar couldn't help thinking, *what good's a brain without a heart?*

The farther he went, the colder he became, until a brisk

chill surrounded him. Could Sebastian really have gone down here? He rubbed his hands together to keep warm, but a breeze chilled him to the bone. That's when he realized he had exited the tunnel and now stood within a great cavernous space. He looked high up into the shadows. His foot suddenly slipped from under him, and the world flipped upside down.

Edgar landed on his back with a big *oof!*—the wind knocked out of him. His face must have been bright red.

He let the shock settle, and then rolled onto his hands and knees. He attempted to stand, but his arms shot out in either direction. His face smacked the ground—if it wasn't red before, it certainly was now.

He glanced into the distance, now aware of the icy floor of the cavern, which spread far into the shadows, glowing. A bit more careful, he scrambled to his feet. This time, instead of walking, he bent his knees, kept his feet flat against the ice, and pushed with all his might.

Edgar skated forward about ten feet before losing momentum. He bent his knees, summoned his strength, and lunged forward, this time skating twice as far. A smile lit up his face the likes of which he'd never known before.

Suddenly, the cold was a non-issue. Edgar found himself skating merrily across an endless sheet of ice in the great cavernous space. His breath billowed in his face in quick, crystalline clouds. His arms became flailing balance beams, his feet a set of ice skates.

"Hello!" Edgar called out.

"*Hello*!" his voice echoed in response. *Hel-lo-lo-lo…*

"Wee!" he shouted, spinning in wild circles.

"*Wee-ee-ee…*"

"Woo!"

"Woo-oo-oo…"

He was having so much fun skating and playing on the ice that he did not notice the first, second, or even third warning sign proclaiming:

DANGER: OPEN CHASM

Centuries of disregard had left the signs withered and practically illegible, and although softly illuminated by the ice, the space remained quite dark. So, he was not necessarily to blame, and yet he managed after a few really good lunges to bring himself terribly near the edge of a deep, bellowing, seemingly endless drop-off.

Edgar swung his leg forward and yelled out, "Yippee!"

before slipping to his rump a second time, which he rode to a stop.

This time his voice did not echo back. Instead, a loud, teeth-grinding grumble sounded, followed by a split-second of silence, and an ear-shattering crash exploded in the distance.

Glacier. The word and the image of a massive ice hunk shimmered in his mind. He'd seen it before in the musty pages of *The Iceberg Commeth* by U. Gino Neil. He envisioned the ice webbed with several tiny cracks spreading into open crevices and resulting in a gargantuan shift of snow and ice. He'd caused an avalanche somewhere—he was certain.

"Poppycock," Edgar whispered. There was something different about his voice. It felt heavy.

He repeated a little louder, "Poppycock."

No echo.

He took a deep breath and without regard for ice hunks bellowed, "POPPYCOCK!"

A tiny, inconsequential cracking noise sounded in the distance. However, still no echo. Whatever walls or chasms had bounced his voice back to him before no longer influenced his shouts. He leaned forward, reaching between his outstretched legs, and realized his feet were dangling over the edge of a cliff.

Edgar discovered the soft beveled edge near his ankles.

He fought the urge to panic and pulled his knees up, drawing his feet back onto the ice. An inch a minute, he rolled onto his stomach. He flip-flopped, so that his arms dangled where his feet had been.

He had been able to see the ice because of the soft glow it gave off. Where he lay and behind him, he could still see the flat stretch of mild blue. But before him, where his feet had dangled over open space, he could not even see his hands. It was black—and frighteningly cold.

He groped around the icy floor, locating the smooth edge. He felt along it—it was sturdy as a rock. He slid closer so he could reach even farther down the edge. There was no telling how deep the drop-off was. He misjudged the sturdiness—a fist-sized chunk of ice broke free and tumbled into the abyss. Edgar tensed, keeping perfectly still, and waited for the chunk to hit the bottom.

It didn't.

The cold had numbed his fingertips. He lay there, the

adrenaline wearing off. He cast his gaze to the side and saw a long, wide edge extending a soft blue line in the dark open space. It was not a smooth edge as he had initially thought; it was jagged and rough—a line, sure, but not a smooth one. He had not seen the signs, but now he knew: OPEN CHASM.

Edgar slowly inched away from the edge, a painstaking process. He had to dig his toes into the ground and pull his body with his feet. The effort caused a sharp, deafening pain in his head, a nagging, insistent pressure that filled his ears with a medium-pitched whine.

A small price to pay, Edgar thought. Horrified of heights, he was not going to risk tumbling into an endless abyss, thank you very much. He'd take the headache and the noise over that sort of end any day.

The noise rose steadily. He realized as the pain spread throughout his body that he was not experiencing a headache. The ground rumbled. The whine rose to an ear-rattling pitch. Edgar gave a start. The motorized whir was coming from the chasm. An image of the wispy gray fog flashed in his mind, and his words, "Do you mean *factory* machine parts?"

The motorized whir hit him with tremendous force. Whatever it was, it was suddenly right there! Edgar curled into a ball and shielded his ears. The din was excruciating, and he was paralyzed beneath it.

The sound cut off without warning and wound down to an empty machine rattle. There was a *click*, and a bright yellow spotlight shone down on him.

A symphony of crashing ice chunks echoed from all directions, revealing the true limitlessness of the space. It may well have been the center of the earth it was so vast. Edgar got out of his ball. There was no one to save him now, no one for miles. He stood—shaking—and faced the light.

10

THE MACHINE TECHNICIAN

The spotlight beamed down on him. Before, in the dark, Edgar had been able to make out the sleek glow of the ice. Standing in the beam of the yellow spotlight, he could see nothing more than yellow-green splotches. The machine whir ceased—its engine must have cut off—but the battery powering the spotlight hummed noticeably.

He considered running. He could turn right around and skate off into the distance. But he'd be caught. Whatever was attached to the other side of that spotlight had risen from a considerable depth at warp speed. And if not warp speed, a speed quicker than his legs could manage on the ice.

Edgar stood as tall as he could. In his firmest voice, he

called out, "Hello there! I couldn't help but notice—your light is shining right in my face!"

He listened to the electric hum of the spotlight battery for a few moments, wondering if he had been heard at all. Finally, there was another *click!*, and he thought he heard a squeal.

What on Earth? He thought. *Surely, I must be imagining things.*

The bright yellow beam powered down, fading to a dim glow. A giant metal platform materialized right before him. It had a spotlight across its thick rail.

There was another soft squeal, followed by an impromptu snort.

Edgar squinted in disbelief. *Can't be.*

It was.

Standing atop the platform was a stout, broad-shouldered figure who had the knobby, fleshy head of a warthog. Edgar had never seen a person like him before. At the front of his mouth, where his narrow jaw and protruding lips formed a snout, two beveled molars jutted straight out. The man held two tall levers extending from the platform in his pink fists. He wore a dark and filthy flak jacket, matching pants, and his wide feet were dressed in big black boots.

He remained silent except for the occasional snort or squeal. His heavy breathing indicated a perpetual nervousness, and when he glanced in Edgar's direction, it was with a look of trepidation.

"Who are you?" Edgar called out.

The warthog man studied him. He pulled back on one of the levers. A clicking sound repeated twice, then a soft rattle started up—much gentler than the noise that had assaulted Edgar as the machine rose up from the chasm—and the platform lowered to the ice.

The Warthog man stood blinking on the platform, his chubby hands wrapped around the tall levers. He wrinkled his nose, giving another snort.

"Thank you for dimming the light," Edgar said, trying to be courteous. He did not know what to make of this fellow. He wondered whether he even spoke English; so far he'd only managed a few snorts and the occasional squeal.

Edgar waited while the fellow eyeballed him. He was going to have to make the first move. He pulled back his shoulders, sucked in his stomach, and approached the platform.

He got about five feet when the warthog man backed off of the levers and squealed mightily. Edgar threw his arms up in defense.

The warthog squealed uncontrollably. His hulking body bounced around the rails on the platform, unable to flee. He twisted his nose in disgust, as if he'd just seen a large rat walking across the floor. After a while, he tired, resting his arms and gasping for breath.

Edgar had scared him, was all. He kept his distance until the warthog's squeals softened to breathless snorts.

But it was the warthog who spoke first—in a voice that sounded like gravel. "Don't you know not to sneak up on people?"

"Beg your pardon?" Edgar couldn't believe it—sneak up on *him*. *He* had risen from the deep in a large, frightening machine that emitted an incapacitating whine, a machine so loud it caused massive ice hunks to dislodge from the cavern and smash to the ground, a machine that had traveled the depths of the abyss in seconds, stopped suddenly, and shone a blinding spotlight in his face. Just how, Edgar wanted to know, had *he* snuck up on *him*?

The warthog man's chest rose mightily, paused, then dropped. He had a wide, muscular torso beneath a broad layer of fat. Edgar had come to know one thing from his Uncle Warnock, that the wrong kind of weight—meaning fat—caused many problems, such as difficulty breathing, sometimes a throat whistle, excessive sweating, and a thing mysterious to Edgar that Uncle Warnock referred to on several occasions as *die-beeties*. Although his uncle drew no sympathy from him, *this* fellow was of a different disposition; there was gentleness in his face, a longing for companionship, the look of a fellow who spent long hours alone in the dark. Edgar could certainly relate to that.

"I'm sorry I frightened you," Edgar said.

"You didn't frighten me," he snapped.

Edgar thought of the squealing dance he'd evoked when approaching him the first time—if that wasn't frightened, he didn't know what was. "Well, I certainly wasn't trying to sneak up on you." Edgar cast his gaze along the gigantic rig, even though the shadows obscured it. "What is this machine, by the way? It's quite large."

"Oh, quite large," the warthog man replied, suddenly full of excitement. "It's the biggest one here."

"The biggest one here?"

"That's what I said; are you deaf?"

Edgar was appalled.

The warthog lowered his head. "I didn't mean that," he said. "Been a long time since there's been people down here. You forget how to deal with 'em."

"Don't worry," Edgar said. "I know how you feel."

The warthog man struggled to find the right words.

Edgar spoke first. "This machine—is it really the biggest one?"

The fellow perked up. "Oh, yes, definitely." Then his shoulders sunk, and he said in a softer voice, "Well, not the *absolute* biggest. But it's the second biggest, for sure."

"And what does it do?"

"What does it do? Many things, many things."

"Oh," Edgar replied.

"Consider it like this: we're in a factory, right?"

"Right."

"And it's a big ole factory, isn't it?"

"It is."

"And one thing you should know is that every big factory's got to have some very particular things to keep it goin'—after all, that's how the inventors made it, to keep functionin' alright."

Edgar nodded. Only the warthog man's gravelly voice filled the cavern now.

"So, every factory's got to have EMPs—that's Essential Machine Parts, a highly technical term. *This*," he said, pointing to his rig, "is the heart. Every one of the factories they built's got a heart."

"Excuse me," Edgar said. "But did you say that the inventors made this place?"

"Aye, and fine work, too."

"And, sorry for sounding dense, but didn't you say factor*ies*—plural—as in, more than one factory?"

"That's right. You're a quick one. An' like I was sayin', this is the heart o' the factory. Come here—I'll show you."

He extended his arm, motioning for Edgar to join him on the platform. Edgar studied the heavy-looking metal crossbars encircling the man. The spotlight had dimmed to a soft glow, lighting the immediate structural components of the machine, but falling short of capturing the entire rig.

Beyond the platform, massive steel girders and thick corrugated pipes disappeared into the dark.

"Have a better look." He reached down low to another set of levers and pulled on a few of them. There was a *click*, and the spotlight beamed on full. "Onto the platform," he urged.

Edgar stepped onto the platform, and he sealed them in by closing a small metal gate. Adjusting various levers and wheels, he brought the spotlight around and shone it back across the rigging. A vast copper-plated armor lit up. This side of the machine must have been thirty feet tall and a hundred feet wide, practically an entire building in size. Each of the copper plates stood taller than either Edgar or the warthog man, and there were hundreds of them shielding the machine. A gaping hole remained open down low on the rig, out of which protruded a heavy steel arm connecting to the platform. As the light shone across the hole, the inner workings were revealed: a hundred resting pistons, well-oiled cogs, gears, sprockets, and an entire network of corrugated pipes.

"Whoa!" Edgar shouted, unable to contain his surprise. "It's magnificent."

Beaming, the warthog man grinned between two jutting molars, saying, “Yes it is, yes it is.”

“What does a heart do?”

“The heart? Why, the heart’s gotta give energy to the rest of the place.”

“Where does the energy come from?” Edgar asked.

“Raw materials, of course.”

“What raw materials?”

“Well, er, materials like sludge.” The warthog’s face filled with sadness. “Didn’t used to be sludge … used to be we never heard of such an awful disgusting thing. Used to burn natural gas in the fire pits. Natural gas is clean, pure, efficient.”

“What happened?”

“Things changed. The waters turned black, thick. Jus’ terrible—still gives me the shivers. And gas ran out. But what can you do? You adapt to the changes. You figure a way to use the sludge. And we did that. So the sludge gets channeled into troughs … then moved into fire pits. Energy gets created.”

Edgar suddenly thought of Uncle Warnock’s voice in the hollow before the mechanical mantises had tried to thrash him to pieces. "Careful with that hose," he'd commanded. "Line up the hoses with the troughs. Watch the sludge!" He shivered at the thought.

"But the energy's no good unless it goes someplace," the warthog continued. "And there's lots of places it needs to go to make a factory this size operate. So, this baby gathers all the energy and transmits it to the rest of the place—just like a heart pumps blood to the whole body, so this machine pumps energy to all the rooms and stations."

"And how does it 'pump' energy?"

The warthog man grinned. "I thought you'd never ask—hold on."

He took hold of the larger lever and pushed it forward. A heavy motor started up, grumbling and rattling, coughing out white billowy clouds. The spotlight clicked off, leaving them in complete darkness. Edgar had no idea what was happening.

The warthog man yelled above the noise, "Hold onto your butt!"

Without warning, he cranked the other large lever forward, and the entire outer wall of the machine began to glow. The glow intensified, forming a blinding blue aura.

Suddenly an ear-shattering explosion rocked the machine, and a pulse of energy shot straight toward the ceiling, causing the entire cavern to quake and rain down hunks of ice.

As the pulse disappeared through the ceiling high above, the ice shower ceased, and the explosive sound diminished, no longer obscuring the grumbling noise of the machine, and Edgar stared off into space. A realization had just hit him like a fist. "The trembling room!"

The warthog touched Edgar's shoulder and yelled, "Did you say something?"

Edgar shook his head.

"Best hold onto your butt again—we're going in."

He didn't like the sound of "we're going in." Edgar shouted, "*Where* are we going?"

But the warthog man already had his hands around the appropriate levers, and with one final adjustment, there was a giant burst of steam and the entire machine shot into the cavern.

Edgar tried to scream.

The machine plummeted down the endless cavern at warp speed, a long horrible whine issuing out from somewhere inside the gargantuan rig. But the sound was not so unsettling as the hollow feeling in his gut as they plunged into the abyss. Edgar's screams disappeared into thin air. All he could do was hold onto the rail for dear life. And he could not help but think what would happen to a machine of this size when it crashed into the bottom.

They descended for what felt like hours, the wind whipping his face, his grip tiring, his throat dry. He began to wonder if the chasm even had a bottom.

Just when Edgar thought his guts would implode, and his thin body would get sucked out into the void, he felt a rough hand around his shoulder, holding him down. A loud hiss rang out, steam bursting from a gigantic pipe. The plummeting machine pulled up as if the airbrake had been engaged, and Edgar's guts returned to their original position.

The noise caught up to him, blasting an awful whine. The machine slowed to a complete stop, and the warthog man cut the engine. It rattled for another minute as small quakes shook the massive copper-plated body before dissipating. And only a mild ringing persisted in Edgar's ears, although his hands gripped the rail for dear life.

Shuffling in place, the warthog man kicked on the spotlight.

The yellow beam lit up a cracked marble floor and what looked like the entrance to a grand ballroom. Edgar shivered; he could see his breath.

"Where are we?" he whispered.

The warthog squealed and proceeded to open the gate on the platform. He ushered him onto the hard marble floor. "I know who you are," the warthog said.

His face bore no more timidity. He was resolute and sharp. His wet pointy snout quivered. "I knew it was you. I heard rumors, and I didn't doubt they was true."

"Who am I?"

"Edgar Noone, of course."

"Edgar Noone?"

The warthog man secured himself onto the platform behind the gate. "Who else?" he said.

"Where have you taken me?"

"Where you wanted to go."

"But I didn't tell you I wanted to go anywhere."

The warthog gave a snort. He struggled to breathe he

was so anxious. "Don't you dream? Don't you ever see without seeing? Or talk without speaking?"

"I don't know what you mean," Edgar cried.

Suddenly the man was reflective. "This machine—used to be a powerful heart. Used to keep things pure. Used to do its big brother proud. Ain't good for much these days 'cept moving around the caverns and chambers, sending energy that don't run nothing. The big machine—now *that* was something. Still is, even though it hasn't worked to serve its real purpose in years. You should know; you've seen it."

Edgar felt confused. "I haven't … have I?"

"Used to be a glorious thing. Before the Darkness, anyway." Great sadness consumed him. "But it is what it is. And the world is all the poorer for it."

"The world? I don't understand."

"Look to your dreams, young Edgar. Trust your mind, and trust your instincts. You will find the answers there. I heard reports of the other factories—that they was still in workin' order and keepin' the world good, safe, clean. Some other young folks like yourself are all that's left to stop the world from goin' the way of this factory. And you can't do it alone, even though yeh want to. I can tell you want to."

The warthog man dug inside his trousers and removed a crumpled envelope.

"Here," he said, sticking the envelope in Edgar's direction. "Your parents were good people. They never would have let things get this way. They wouldn't have stood for it."

Edgar took the envelope; it no longer felt like paper, it was so old—it was as soft as cloth.

"Mr. Warthog, I don't understand."

"Look, there's horrible things out there in the world. The beast minion IT still looks for yeh. Its boss can't come and get you, though—and he wants to real bad, I guarantee. But you ain't getting *out* neither, with the factory pulling against it."

"How is the factory pulling against that?"

"Some of us workers here, we jes' keep the rigs in order and runnin' the bes' we can. This here heart does its duty. The brain's what's in decay—that glorious thing you dream about. But the soul's the real problem. The soul—the essence—is jus' as alive as you and me, and it used to be good, but it is what the factory is, and now that the darkness has consumed the place, the soul is dark, too. It's up to you to figure out the rest. Just keep in mind—HIM'S out there, too. If yeh have to go out, you'll have to be careful. I don't envy you, that's for sure—but I believe in you. Lots of us do." The warthog man clicked the spotlight off, leaving Edgar in the dark, and he started the gargantuan machine.

"Mr. Warthog, wait!" Edgar shouted, but he knew it was useless. Then it hit him. He shouted, "Stewpot says hello!"

The awful whine started up, and the machine thrust off the ground, rocketing high above him, reaching somewhere far into the dark, its whine fading quickly, the rumbling vibrations softening to nothing.

Edgar's head was swimming. His journey to escape this evil place had uncovered more truths than he'd ever imagined or hoped. And to think, *he* was at the center of it all. The visions returned. The machine of copper-plated globes, magnificent and pure, built by inventors, his parents—the brain. He pictured the Banyan tree turning colors, too—the place he'd been born, before the dark factory and his life there.

But something else, too—something terrible. A stranger in a cloak, covering Edgar's face with a blindfold and dragging him through the halls. Only to awaken in his room feeling cold, drained, and frightened.

Edgar brushed his fingers across the soft crumpled envelope. He didn't know what it contained, but he felt security in its presence. A slight burning in his pocket reminded him of the pouch. He reached in to touch the plush velvet bag; it, too, was soft.

Another image came to him: the factory. He saw it from afar. Thick blankets of smog surrounded its smokestacks. The black river oozed through the ashen ground, gurgling. But, the awful sky disappeared, replaced by a vibrant sunset. Edgar smiled—*he* had created that.

He cleared the images from his mind and walked toward the entrance of a grand ballroom. He focused on his friend's advice, that looks were *not* what one should trust in this place.

Ever since the factory had come under the influence of the mysterious Darkness, it had come under a spell. And Edgar knew very little about spells—books on the topic were few—but he had discovered in the past few days that the mystery of the ice was just a property of a grand spell. And spells had only as much power as the one under its influence allowed. Once he realized this, the goose bumps on his flesh went away. His breath stopped forming frozen cloudbursts. The air became pleasant.

A couple of torch lights flickered into being, lighting up the grand façade of the ballroom entrance. Its two austere wooden doors creaked open, shedding clouds of dust and debris, revealing a massive room glowing amid the warmth of two dozen torch lights along a colonnade. Plush red drapes hung from a high-up ceiling.

Edgar stood in the entrance, basking in the orange glow of the ballroom. Except for a long red carpet, the room was empty. This he knew to be a spell far stronger than wooden doors and hovering threes, for many years his cold cement room had taught him to be wary of the most dangerous of all spells—a spell called comfort.

Clenching the soft crumpled envelope, feeling for the plush velvet pouch, he stepped forward into the room. A gust slammed the doors shut behind him, sealing him there.

Edgar didn't even flinch.

11

THE MAN WITH MANY TUBES

Edgar stood in the empty ballroom and wondered at all the fuss made over names. The warthog man called him Edgar Noone without ever having been properly introduced. Noone—just like the little wooden door with the sign he'd misread: NOONE SHALL ENTER. The friendly dust bunnies told him of a boy named Edgar Noone, descended from a long line of inventors, who was rumored to be a light of hope in the perpetual and seemingly everlasting darkness spread throughout the factory. Hadn't his friend Sebastian assured him there was great power in his name? Noone didn't feel right, though.

Edgar Noone … Edgar Noone … Edgar Noone.

The more he said it, the more foreign it sounded. The name may have gotten him through the first door, but nothing felt more natural to him than Edgar Trunk. Yes, *he* was Edgar Trunk. Nothing against this Noone kid—Edgar suddenly felt more power in Trunk than he ever did in any other word or name. He'd stick to it, thank you very much.

He looked ahead of him in the flickering light of a dozen torches. He was not alone in the grand ballroom. A long banquet table had materialized. It stretched down the middle, stocked with a dozen platters of food. And the aroma! Divine. Just divine.

Edgar looked upon the treats displayed to him. One platter with honey-glazed ham cut into pink juicy slices. Another platter of deviled eggs. One of fresh cut melon and strawberries. A cheesy potato casserole. A chocolate meringue pie. A piping hot tray of double-fudge brownies covered in chocolate icing. On and on. He passed each dish with delight, the aroma distinct and rich, lingering only until he moved on to the next, where he was greeted with another decadent scent.

Edgar's mouth salivated. His tongue grew eager, licking at his lips and watering. If he could just perhaps taste a sliver or a morsel…

His outstretched fingers paused inches from a quivering mound of fresh whipped cream. A bowl of strawberries sat next to it, glistening and plump.

He could not touch them. He could not. Edgar continued along the table, moving deeper into the ballroom. Small ivory candles dripped onto the red table runner. Beyond a spread of juicy meats and a full-size turkey, there was another temptation that drew Edgar to a full stop.

Cheese.

Thirteen assorted wedges of rich, pungent smelling cheeses. Gouda, stilten, roquefort, feta, mozzarella, manchego, humboldt fog, brie. They were all there, and they were splendid. An assault on the senses. A war on the taste buds. He had to try them. The urge was too great to resist.

Edgar reached down greedily, his dirty fingernails digging into the soft body of a brie wedge. He brought the wedge to his mouth, held it there to delight in its odor. The taste buds were overwhelmed; a thin salivary strand escaped his lips, dropping onto the tablecloth. It smelled so wonderful! Yes, now … now he was ready.

He opened wide and plopped the cheese wedge into his mouth, expecting a taste of pure heaven.

So sorry, but it was a wretched spell.

What he expected to taste was the smooth, salty, buttery creaminess of brie with that ever so slight tartness of the white outer layer. What he tasted instead was the pasty, bitter texture of candle wax with an ever so slight tinge of dust.

"Blah!" he shouted, ejecting the chewed wax in a spray. It left a horrible residue in his mouth.

He stood back to observe an even more horrific sight.

At the head of the table, enthroned in a high-backed and ornate wooden chair, sat an old, old man. He wore a thick metal cap, from which protruded thirty or more tubes—all a sickly white rubber. The tubes cascaded down the chair and on top of, beneath, and around the long banquet table. Edgar daren't look at them, for the old man studied him closely, and he did not want to get caught staring. He thought it most polite to just maintain eye contact. But the old man's face caused Edgar to grimace. It was a deathly, sickly face the color of light gray. The nose, long and crooked, hung at an unbalanced angle. His neck and arms were a resting place for liver spots. And his eyes—oh, his eyes caused Edgar to shudder twice. They were pale and empty, with a tapestry of black veins webbed across the whites of them.

Even the pupils had a haunting and desperate quality—one of them bulged large and black, fully dilated, while the other was hardly a pin dot.

He spoke in a voice wet and throaty, with the hint of amusement.

"Do you eat the white?"

"What do you want?" Edgar asked.

The old man wrenched his face into the nearest smile he could achieve. "You are a smart one. I can tell. I *feel* it. But tell me, do you eat the white?"

Edgar did not like the question. He considered it, wondering where the trick lay.

"I refer to the cheese, of course," the man said. "Brie is a lovely cheese. The King of cheeses, in fact. So did you like it?"

Edgar's face twisted in disgust. "It wasn't cheese at all," he said. "It was awful."

"Yes, well, I'm afraid it's the best we can do with what we've got. Not mature, anyway. Real brie cheese is a rich brown—the white, I'm afraid, is only the result of stabilizing ingredients meant to allow the safe transport of cheese across the world. But I can see that I bore you. You're a young boy; you have no interest in fine cheese. You just love the *smell* of it. Very well, have some more."

The man extended his hand toward the assortment of cheeses. Edgar didn't dare look. The sight of the man's arm, dripping with loose skin, speckled with a million dark brown liver spots, turned his stomach. The taste of wax still lingered in his teeth, a ready reminder of the spell cast around him. Edgar stepped back. "It isn't cheese. It's a trick."

"My, my," the man said. "You are not to be fooled, I can see. Spells are for children, I admit. For children and for those whose minds are simple like children—I'm afraid their number are many. Very well, then."

With that, the old man snapped his bony fingers, and the lovely feast crumbled away to a pile of rubble and dust, revealing not the strong construction of a table made of oak, but rather the dark and intricate workings of a machine to which the many tubes connected the old, old man.

Wheels turned, pistons jumped, steam burst from the rigging in small gray clouds. Edgar jumped away from it as though the dials and pistons would burn him. A dark green liquid moved through the tubes. He noticed one detail he had overlooked, and his blood ran cold.

The old, old man cackled. "You see … the truth is never so pretty."

Many of the tubes ran from the man's helmet to the machine, connecting at some knobby metal joint. Others ran deeper inside, appearing through the glass of small containers lining the bottom half of the machine. Inside the glass, Edgar made out the stiff bodies of Crillows. They were bound inside by their necks, and smaller versions of the old man's helmet had been fastened to their tiny bird heads. As far as he could tell, they were dead. Just like the Crillows he had spotted in the pathless wood, those bound inside the machine appeared lifeless and unmoving, their wings cocked at an awkward angle.

"What are you doing to them?" Edgar cried.

The sound of a child's voice in distress sent goose pimples up and down the old man's limbs. His face was a permanent grimace of amusement now. "The machine needs life," he bellowed maniacally. "You must think it so easy to keep a place like this going. You must think it a trifle of effort. But I assure you there is nothing trifling about its purpose."

Edgar trembled. "I don't see what killing those nice birds has to do with the machine."

"Life, my boy. Life. You think sludge and a silly pig's machine can keep all of this going? I can tell you it's not so simple."

"I know who you are," Edgar said angrily. He knew little about the machine, and even less about 'this place,' and yet he felt suddenly very passionate about rebuking this ghastly menace before him.

"Who am I, then?" he replied, delighted.

Edgar recalled the words of many creatures he had met on his journey, and now he declared with fear and determination, "You work for HIM!"

The man with many tubes ceased smiling. A look of anger rose upon his face, and he said with surprising strength, "I work for no one. I am so much more than HIM."

"And Uncle Warnock?"

"Pah! Warnock is a fool," he scoffed. "A fool who couldn't even keep you contained in that fool-proof cell."

The old man waved his hand, and a panel slid back on

the machine, revealing another glass compartment—this one filled with a murky liquid. Suddenly, a head bobbled into view.

"No!" Edgar cried in horror. The face was bloated and pale, but he recognized it at once.

"What do you think of your nice and friendly uncle now?"

"That's not real," Edgar whimpered.

"No need to thank me." The man was too proud.

"He didn't deserve that. No one deserves that. You're just…evil, awful." Edgar wanted to cry.

"Do you know what soul is?"

Edgar stared at the sick face of his uncle, unable to look away.

The man with many tubes glowed with an evil power. "DO YOU KNOW WHAT SOUL IS?"

"I-I don't know what you mean," Edgar stuttered.

"Soul is life, you little boy. And I need life. This place needs life. It cannot exist without it. The world cannot exist without it."

Edgar risked a glance at the narrow chambers containing the lifeless Crillows.

"You see," the old, old man observed. "Life. Knowledge. Experience. Essence. Ah, yes … essence. It is like little fruit candies. I *need* those candies!"

Edgar backed away. "Do you mean to take *my* essence?"

He practically cooed, "Yours has always been the sweetest, my dear boy."

The memory of a cloaked stranger carrying a blindfold flashed in his mind. It all made sense to him now. Edgar felt faint. "I've been here before, haven't I?"

"Don't you recognize it? Oh, right, I forgot. You were too weak to fight my power." He waved his hand and a figure appeared out of thin air, wearing a cloak.

"No," Edgar snapped. "What do you want with me?"

"Your essence, of course ... from one *soul* to another."

The old man snapped his fingers, and the cloaked figure disappeared. "I don't need eyes and ears here, don't need hands, when I've got my own."

"Why didn't you kill me like you did those Crillows? Or Warnock?"

"I wouldn't dream of it," he moaned. "And waste you all in one sitting. Dear boy, you are all that's left in this place that's real. A real delicacy in a world of declining taste." He was fawning now. "Don't look so sad. You are an offering ... by HIM. To keep this place running while his hideous influences pervaded the walls, I had a fee. I agreed to let him do whatever he wished—his big master plan, superfluous really—in exchange for you. He needs me, you know. His plan will not succeed without my cooperation." The old, old man smiled wryly. "If he knew you were still alive, he'd be *very* unhappy—dare I say, afraid. But as I said, I wasn't going to finish you hastily. How foolish *that* would have been! A delicacy deserves to be savored—sipped over time. Don't you agree?"

"I don't understand."

"No? I think you do."

Edgar wanted to turn and run. He wanted more than anything to be gone from this place and this journey and to never have seen the things he had seen. The cloaked stranger blindfolding him had been real. His notions of being dragged through the corridors made sense—how his memory of it ended abruptly, mere pieces leftover from having his essence feasted upon. Who knew how many times *he* had been inside that machine, with tubes attached to *his* head.

"Stay away from me," Edgar growled. "I don't like you."

"*You don't like me*—so sad," he mocked. "Where will you go? Do you think you can make it out of here without my help? That is what you want, isn't it? You're always talking about it. Always dreaming. I admit, I've savored that, too—those wistful fantasies of yours about the machine. The brain, you call it. Well, it is nothing without me. It's hardly anything now."

Edgar kept his eyes on the man with many tubes as he backed away, but he knew the man was right. Doors mysteriously closing, spells deceiving his eyes and nose, the cloaked stranger, his evil magic—he was at the mercy of this vile villain.

"Very well," the man shouted. "I will have to enjoy the dessert before the dinner."

Edgar didn't know what he meant, but within moments he saw … and his heart stopped cold in his chest.

Appearing all of a sudden, just as the food had appeared and disappeared upon the long banquet table, one of the narrow slots opened up, and hovering above it as if held by an invisible brace, floundered the very last Crillow on the island, his friend Sebastian.

"No!" Edgar cried. "Leave him alone!"

As if by a force of magic, the man held out his gnarly hand and swirled his finger round and round in little circles, causing Sebastian to spin in the air.

Sebastian cried out; his voice was unmistakable. "No, please, no—don't hurt me!"

Edgar stopped backing away and instead rushed toward the machine. When he was within ten feet, the man boomed, "STOP! You cannot save him."

Edgar didn't care what he could or could not do. He went right to his friend with arms outstretched. He would snatch him right out of the air and flee as fast as he could. If anyone knew the secret halls and tunnels it was Sebastian; *he* would lead them to safety.

But as he reached the edge of the machine, he slammed into an invisible barrier, coming to a sudden and complete stop. He may as well have hit a concrete wall.

The old, old man gave another maniacal cackle; he was

enjoying this immensely. "Don't waste your energy, boy. It is useless."

"It's not useless," Edgar cried through a visage of frustration and anger.

The ancient and decrepit hand paused, and Sebastian came to a stop upside down. He hung at an awkward angle, but by now he could make out the presence of his friend Edgar, and when he realized it truly was the boy, his face twisted into an awful frown. "Young Sir!" he hollered. "Get away from this place."

"Sebastian, I won't leave you. I'll find a way to get you down."

"No, it's useless. You've got to get out of here," Sebastian cried.

The man with many tubes grinned. "Listen to your friend," he said. "He is wise."

"Be quiet!" Edgar quipped.

"Such passion. The stupid bird race would have lasted ten times longer had they a fraction of the emotion you've got. Crillows! Wretched, simple creatures—the world will not miss your kind."

"Please, Edgar," Sebastian pleaded.

Edgar didn't know what to do. He tried again to move closer to his friend but was halted by that invisible wall. He stepped sideways and approached from a different angle—same impenetrable wall.

"Sebastian, what shall I do?"

"Young Sir, it is useless. Do you know who this is?"

Edgar couldn't find the words fast enough, and the man with many tubes cried out blissfully, "Tell us, stupid bird; tell us all who I am."

For a moment, Sebastian found Edgar's face, and they locked gazes for a prolonged sigh of desperation, hopelessness, and fear. Finally, a defeated Crillow responded, "He is the Factory. He is the Vessel."

"The Vessel! Ladies and Gentlebird, we have a winner," the man with many tubes howled. "The Vessel. Well, we've covered that already, dumb Crillow. You haven't been listening this whole time. Nevertheless, I need to be filled."

The old man lifted his palm; a wave of loose skin rippled under his arm. Out of nowhere appeared one of those tiny bird-sized helmets with the tubes. It slowly approached Sebastian's head and fitted itself right on top with ease. Sebastian squirmed, but the old man's magical grip on him was tight.

With a flick of the wrist, a small pulse of energy shot from the inside of the long machine up through Sebastian's helmet, and his neck went rigid. A low, painful whine escaped his taut beak.

"No!" Edgar shouted. This time he found the invisible wall and pounded it with his fists, hammering as hard and furiously as he could. Only, it was all for naught. A bright green fluid began to run from Sebastian's helmet through the tubes, working its way into the machine.

Moments later, the green substance appeared on the other side of the rigging, this time working its way in little pulses toward the old man's helmet. The man with many tubes, the factory's Vessel, jolted back in ecstasy, awaiting his prize with the utmost delight.

Edgar was horror-bound. The green fluid, the vibrant essence of his dear friend, inched up the tubes, where an electrified old man, a vessel for receiving the stolen souls of others, awaited it. Edgar could watch no longer.

He charged the throne, bringing his hands before him like small weapons. The man, so engrossed in the moment, did not even see him. Edgar acted so quickly, so ferociously and desperately, that he did not know what he would do until he had done it. And with a long despairing cry, he leapt toward the old, ashy, gray corpse figure connected to the machine, and he seized the nearest tube in his hands. Then, driven by fear and madness, he bit down on the milky white rubber, chomping with all the might and fury in his soul.

Years of eating hardened stale bread rolls had strengthened both Edgar's jaws and his teeth, and so when he bit down on the tube, it gave easily. He severed the hose. Before anyone could react, Edgar reached up and gripped two more tubes. Clenching a sour, gnarly hunk of hose in his mouth, he yanked at the other hoses with all his might.

They broke free of the helmet with two distinct pops!

The man with many tubes realized what was happening, but Edgar had already taken two more tubes and popped them off of his rigging. Seeing what had happened, seeing Edgar's frantic, determined, horrified face, he became rigid with anger. He lifted his strongest arm and struck the boy across the face. Edgar spun to the floor.

The old, old man gathered his severed tubes before the

essence he had drawn went to waste. But it was too late. The damage that had been done was severe, and Sebastian no longer remained in his magical death grasp. In fact, the Crillow was nowhere to be seen.

Edgar, blinded for a few moments by the force of the menacing blow, felt about the cold floor. When he could see again, and gazed across the room, he saw that the spell had been completely broken. The red carpet had vanished. He no longer lay in a grand ballroom filled with the warm glow of torches. The drapes had gone. The marble pillars, and the orange torch lights had been replaced with a dozen sick yellow bulbs. Where he lay was a great big cell like the one he'd called his bedroom for so many years.

Then he remembered the terrible old man.

Before he could scramble to his feet, the awful menace's voice boomed, "You stupid, stupid boy! You wretched bird! I'll have your dreams *and* your souls—mark my words!"

Edgar spun around, searching for Sebastian. The bird wasn't there! Had he found a grave inside one of the small chambers in the machine? Edgar turned back, but was caught by the old man's stare. The black veins in his eyes spread, bulging. Anger filled his pasty face with darkness. He looked as if he would soon jump from his throne and strangle the boy with those awful liver-spotted hands.

One of the tubes Edgar had pulled free ejected a small amount of essence in a misty spray, whipping about like a snake, before coming to a stop. That was all the machine had managed to extract from his friend. That was it.

"Stupid, stupid boy," the man with not so many tubes raged. He clearly did not function to the fullest of his powers without all his tubes. Somehow, the machine had kept him alive. He needed the machine just as the machine needed to suck the essence from live captives. Edgar wondered how long the man would last now. He made the mistake of stepping closer to observe the Vessel's dwindling power, and it lashed out with his finger and held him in an invisible fist.

Edgar felt it tighten around his abdomen, squeezing the breath out of him.

"No," Edgar whispered.

The man made one final grimace of amusement. Even now he drew pleasure from his work. The more Edgar squirmed, and the bluer his lips turned, the more rapturous the man with many tubes became.

Edgar found himself agreeing, *stupid boy ... you stupid, stupid boy.*

As a dark tunnel encircled his vision, Edgar thought himself to be experiencing hallucinations. This is it, he thought. Now I will die. He saw the spirit of his friend Sebastian rise above the menacing dream stealer's shoulder.

Hello, my friend, he thought. Soon, we will be together.

The hallucination reached down and seized one of the old, old man's many tubes, where he bit it in two.

Edgar instantly felt the grip weaken. He could breathe again. His vision came back.

His bird friend bit another tube in half, and this time Edgar collapsed to the ground, coughing, sucking in air, and the terrible wet and throaty voice of the old man cried out in rage, "You beast! This isn't happening!"

Edgar looked up to see that he had not been hallucinating after all. The spirit of his friend Sebastian remained. He had severed almost all of the man's tubes. The menacing villain writhed on his throne. Now free of many of the tubes, his head jerked wildly about. The transparent gray irises had gone completely black. His evil eyes bulged from his head, and his hands were much weaker now, much slower to thrash about. Edgar, enthralled in the horrific sight, felt a sharp poke in his left calf—Sebastian was trying to get his attention.

"Sebastian," Edgar cried. "You're alive!"

"Yes, I'm alive, Young Sir. Now let's flee this place. Now that the Vessel is gone, IT and HIM will have free reign."

"But IT is dead. And now the Vessel."

"No, Young Sir; IT lives. IT cannot die."

"But how?"

"I can't explain," Sebastian quipped. "Just trust me. We are not safe here."

Sebastian hopped across the room, and Edgar followed. He had so many questions, so many feelings. Behind him, the awful figure of the man with many tubes had begun to turn to ash and crumble away.

The sick yellow bulbs flickered. Edgar felt a fear unlike any he'd ever experienced. He found his feet and ran, moving so quickly Sebastian had trouble keeping up. Edgar instinctively dived toward the far wall, finding a lever in the shadows.

He opened the hidden door, and they were gone from the room forever, not quite free from darkness, but free from a thing Sebastian had called the Vessel and the warthog had called the soul, part living/part machine, that fed upon the lifeblood of the island's creatures, a thing that had stolen his essence in small quantities just to appease an insatiable appetite and a dark will, a thing so vile that Edgar would never forget it.

12

EDGAR PAINTS A DOOR

So fast and fearful was his escape from the Vessel's tomb, that Edgar could only recall flashes of dark tunnels and more grime. He remembered the motorized whir of gates rising and closing. The scent of sour milk and gingersnaps assaulted him on several occasions, while passing hidden grates in the dark. And always, while moving at full-speed, he watched for the evil glow of mechanical red eyes, and listened for the hiss of the evil creature of shadow. At last they came to a small room similar to Storage Closet B, where Edgar had befriended two delightful dust bunnies. Sebastian spoke in a breathless hurry. Fear was still very much with them.

"Young Sir, we have done a very good thing. Do not forget that." Sebastian poked him. "Stand up. I need to show you something."

Sebastian fumbled around in the dark, bumping into Edgar, scraping against the wall. "Ah, here it is," he said. The sound of rusty metal wheels signaled a moving metal flap on the wall that parted from a wide glass window.

Edgar peered out, realizing they were inside some sort of observation room high up in the air. There was enough light for him to see what the room observed: a vast, cosmic space dripping with shadow and murk. Several dark globes filled the room like dead moons in an astral closet. Edgar thought, *This is what Rot looks like. This is what the Darkness is.*

Edgar was solemn. "But this can't be the machine."

"I'm sorry, Young Sir. This is what's become of it."

"But, Sebastian, *the* machine is shiny and brilliant and splendid and…"

"And *good*? Yes, I know. Your parents never dreamed their work would turn to this. Come," Sebastian urged. "We do not have much time. I must go into hiding, and you must flee, or you will never leave this place—you will forever be its prisoner, and the Darkness will consume the world."

Edgar looked upon the rotting machine overtaken by evil, and mourned its once marvelous existence.

"The Vessel is gone," Sebastian said. "He was once a vessel of good, serving to maintain the integrity of this factory. The machine from your dreams, which you saw in rot, was once called the Colossus. It was the Vessel's sole duty to keep the Colossus running. Now the Colossus sleeps. It is useless under the influence of the Darkness. The world suffers each day the Colossus is left in decay, and eventually the world also will turn to rot. But you will discover more about this in time. Just know that the Vessel, while powerful, was bound to this place. It had no real concept of the world. Within the factory walls, it was most powerful, but outside—it had no influence. As the Colossus slept, and the Darkness spread, the Vessel became a vessel of evil. Its only purpose is to the factory—good or evil. And now that the Vessel is gone, there are others who will seek you out. I can't explain it any better, but the Vessel needed you, Edgar. It needed you, and so it made sure that you were kept alive. A junkie and his drug. I suspect a deep forgotten part of him still longed for good over evil, but survival is stronger than all of our most primitive desires. The others will soon know that you are no longer under the protection of the Vessel, and they will seek you out. You are their greatest fear. A mere boy, I know. You will come to find that there is more to Edgar Noone Trunk than broken images and endless halls.

"Fear the hiss from the dark, for it is HIM that leads all evil to your door. If I leave you with one secret, it is this: HIM thinks you are dead. For this very reason you were contained here. But not for long—IT will soon return with news of your survival. I know it's awful, but your stay in these dark walls was for the best. You are not alone in the world. There is much of the world that still remains good—untouched by evil—and you are not the only one who threatens HIM and the Darkness. There are others … at least I hope there are still others. You must find them, Edgar, before the world *is* consumed by this. Follow your heart and follow your mind. I pray it's not too late."

"But, Sebastian, how will I find them? How do we leave this place?"

"Young Sir, you cannot leave this place. *We* cannot leave this place. A very strong spell remains even after the Vessel's death, for in life he was quite powerful. In the wood, you found yourself running for miles without finding the dastardly waters surrounding this island, and yet they are visible from the factory walls. It was a spell that kept you here, imprisoned you on the island, deceived all of your senses."

"I don't understand, Sebastian. Then how will I leave if you say I cannot?"

"Young Sir, sadly I do not have the answer for you. I just feel in my heart that you can."

"And if I can't?"

"If you can't … then we are all doomed. The world is doomed. And all our efforts to thwart HIM and to thwart the spread of Darkness were for nothing."

"Sebastian, please, I don't like to hear you say those things."

"Young Sir, you have been very kind to me. I will miss you."

"Sebastian, don't you dare pull another one of your disappearing tricks."

But he had, in fact, pulled just such a trick. Edgar's friend was gone. He checked the room for a trapdoor and discovered none.

Finally, a voice rang out from the shadows, "Hurry, my friend, for IT draws near. It no longer senses the influence of the Vessel, and now it searches restlessly for you. IT will not return to its master empty-handed."

"Sebastian, wait…"

Silence filled the room.

Edgar basked in it for a long while, reflecting on the words of his friend. So much had happened so quickly, and now he did not know his way. Yet everything was in his hands.

Somewhere in the factory, IT searched for him. Edgar recalled the pitch-black claws, the yellow eyes, the trembling room and his dear friend Stewpot.

And he recalled the other faces, as well. Mr. Harold and Mrs. Margaret, who had been so kind. Sebastian—the bashful Crillow who was ashamed of his feet, whose heart proved biggest and warmest of all. A force of will so strong rose in his gut that he stood at once—resolute, determined.

'Leave this place,' Sebastian had instructed. *Leave this place*, Edgar repeated over and over.

Leave this place … leave this place … leave this place.

Edgar Trunk. Edgar Trunk. Edgar Trunk.

He didn't know where inspiration came from, or what it really was. His life had been so bizarre and defeating. He had lived in fear most of his years, and even now he felt it—a constant edge of fear. He could hone that fear; he could use it to make himself sharp. If there was power in his name, he was not certain how to use it. But he knew one thing: sight could be deceptive.

Edgar took out the small velvet pouch, untied the knot, and let the strings fall to the side. He took a deep breath. This was it.

He opened the pouch. A vibrant rainbow of color erupted from the sack, forming colorful stars upon the ceiling.

Edgar had goose bumps.

He removed the emerald hunk of color, went to the nearest wall, and made a single swipe across it. Then, taking the sapphire hunk, he drew another line. Then a ruby swish.

A diamond slip-slash.

An amber swip-swap.

A hard angle in obsidian.

A fire circle.

Edgar felt alive, empowered. He stood for a moment to

observe the brilliant, sparkling door he had just drawn. The light from his mural covered him in a warm glow. *He* had created this door. Like the sunset before, *he* had the power to change everything. Edgar reached out and gripped the fire orange doorknob he had drawn. It felt warm and firm in his hand—tingly.

The door swung easily open.

At first, Edgar did not believe the view before him. An open door on the factory wall revealed a portal into another place where the Darkness had yet to spread. A gentle breeze entered the room, drawing in from a vast and wondrous expanse of night sky. He had never seen the sky before—at least he did not remember ever having seen it—but he knew and felt in his heart that this was the sky. And all those bright and glittering specks were stars—millions of them, just wonderful!

Edgar stepped through the door—he didn't glance back—and closed the way behind him.

The doorknob vanished from his grip, and when he did finally look around, there was no trace of a door or knob in sight. He had been transported.

It was a cool night. Crisp and alive. Edgar lay down

to take in the magnificent star-filled sky. His heart gave a jump—the moon! This was just as he envisioned it. Edgar rested his head on a plush spongy floor, and as he gazed at the moon and felt the cool breeze against him, and he savored the lovely aroma of fresh-cut grass and honeysuckle, he heard the soft rustle of tree leaves. With a great big smile, he thought with wonder: so this is the world.

Sometime in the night he dozed off. For once, he did not dream, and the smile upon his face seemed to say that was all right by him. Luckily or unluckily, his life *and* his journey had only begun.

In a cottage across the field, a young girl awoke from a fretful dream and turned on her bedroom light. Her name was Olivia Saunders, and she didn't know it yet, but her life was about to become very interesting.

Far away, in a place far darker than the world Edgar had found himself this night, two amber eyes cloaked in a cloud of shadow drifted along the labyrinthine corridors of the factory. A mysterious gust filled the halls, but it was different—empty, hollow.

ABOUT THE AUTHOR

Jason Silva is currently at work on *The Tale of Edgar Trunk: Book 2*, tentatively subtitled *Olivia Saunders and the Stupendous, Eerily Perfect Town (That Was Her Home)...And the Boy Who Wandered There.* He lives with his wife and cat in Los Angeles, CA.

www.EdgarTrunk.com
facebook.com/EdgarTrunk